I0710312

HOBOES, HUSTLERS, AND OUTLAWS

Bad Boys and Macho Men

PETER SCHUTES   J. W. STEED
ADAM MAXWELL BIGGLESWORTH

Four tales of riding rails, selling tail, and sitting in jail

HOBO HONEY - Idaho, a hobo with a hefty hog, struggles to find companionship. Fate sends him Fred, a cherubic youth who can accommodate him completely. Fred proves to be a real teacher, not just teaching Idaho how to be with other men, but even how to be with the man he's always loved.

ON THE BLOCK - In the notorious historically gay neighborhood in downtown Richmond, Virginia known as *The Block,* a young male prostitute, Nick, agrees to an interview he later regrets. He finds solace and companionship with another hustler.

HUSTLER'S LUCK - Rent Boy Frankie gets ribbed by his fellow whores for being a bottom. He doesn't think it's very hard work to do something he loves so much until he meets a *very* challenging trick.

THE FISH - Brandon Little arrives in jail an innocent man. He loses his innocence to Mike Hawk, his gangster cellmate, and a wide variety of other prisoners who appreciate what Brandon can give them.

CONTENTS

Hoboes, Hustlers, and Outlaws - Bad Boys and Macho Men

Copyright © 2024 by Peter Schutes Publishing

All rights reserved.

ISBN: 978-1-963667-12-7

No part of this publication may be reproduced, distributed, or transmitted in any form or by any means, including photocopying, recording, or other electronic or mechanical methods, without the publisher's prior written permission, except as permitted by U.S. copyright law.

The story, all names, characters, and incidents portrayed in this production are fictitious. No identification with actual persons (living or deceased), places, buildings, and products is intended or should be inferred.

Cover Illustration by Kate Chisholm-Woods

This book is for ADULT AUDIENCES ONLY. It contains substantial sexually explicit scenes with multiple partners and graphic language, which may be considered offensive by some readers.

All sexual activity in this work is consensual, and all sexually active characters are 18 years of age or older.

HOBO HONEY

by Peter Schutes

IDAHO

Riding the rails was no life for a beauty like Fred Talmadge. His face was too pretty to be covered in all that soot. Riding from Dallas to St. Louis, he shared a boxcar with a thick hunk of meat named Idaho Jones. Idaho felt protective of the pretty boy with nowhere else to go. Hobos don't get a lot of sex, and when they do, it isn't always mutually consensual. It's almost always with other hobos. No women hang out in the hobo jungles or ride the rails except for a few bull dykes. Idaho preferred women, but only if they preferred him. He hadn't been with a woman in a long time. Freddy was starting to look mighty appealing. But Idaho was a hobo with principles. He would never take advantage of a young soul. But if Fred wanted it, Idaho would happily give it to him.

Idaho was the humble owner of a gigantic cock. Hanging nearly to his knees, the monster, as he called it, was enough to scare away even the most cock-hungry slut out there. He had met a few loose women who could take him halfway. They never walked right afterward.

Fred interrupted Idaho's thoughts. "You got a cigarette, sir?"

"Call me Idaho, son. Yeah, Lucky Strikes means fine tobacco." He held out the pack, and Fred gently removed one cigarette.

"You got a light?"

Idaho chuckled and flicked his Zippo, holding the flame out for Fred to suck. That boy sure had beautiful lips. Idaho would like to kiss him, but he stuck to the code of the road. Fred wasn't making it easy for him, though. The boy held Idaho's hand to steady the flame; the touch of another human being was rare.

"Thanks, Idaho. Damn, your hands are huge!" Fred caressed Idaho's mitts. They were rough against the smooth touch of the young man.

Idaho looked the kid up and down. He had apple cheeks and bright blue peepers. On top of his head was a curly mop of black hair. He had a thin mustache and a scraggly beard so faint you could only see it in the sunlight.

The older hobo felt a stirring in his loins. His gigantic cock swelled involuntarily. He cleared his throat and withdrew his hands. He saw Fred's face fall.

"You don't like me touching you, do you?"

Idaho shook his head. "It's not that. It's complicated."

Fred batted his pretty eyelashes. "Let's uncomplicate things." He reached over and felt for Idaho's cock. He found it and grinned.

"Holy shit, that's thick!"

Idaho nodded, awaiting the inevitable withdrawal of the offer.

"Can I see it?"

This was torture. The kid would probably agree to a hand job, but Idaho liked fucking. This was the reason he rode the rails in the first place. He was so sick of being rejected for being too big. Away from society, it rarely happened. But here it was, and it was happening.

Fred said, "Oh come on, man, I really wanna see it!"

Idaho shrugged. The faster he got this over with, the better. He stood, holding on to the side of the boxcar, and unfastened his overalls, letting them drop. His manhood was half hard, swinging back and forth with the rocking of the train. "There. What do you think?"

Fred's eyes hung open like the jaw of a cartoon cat. "Fucking huge. You're the biggest I ever seen. And I've seen a lot!"

Idaho wanted this hand to fold. "So, can I fuck you?"

Fred pulled out a tub of Vaseline. "I hope there's enough in here!"

The old hobo wasn't expecting things to progress. He didn't want to hurt this frail beauty of a young man. The kid was so eager it confused him. "If you've never seen one so big, what makes you think you can take it?"

Fred put a glob of Vaseline at the base of Idaho's cock and stroked. Soon, the thick meat was glistening. For good measure, the boy spit in his hands to make the cock even more slippery. He spat in his hand and rubbed it on his pink hole. "I had a lot of other stuff in there. Fists and arms. I learned to love it in school. I can take it."

Idaho grew faint as the blood rushed to his cock, which, despite gravity, stuck straight out. It was over a foot long. One in a billion. He grinned at the kid, who smiled back before getting on his knees, his head buried in his arms, giving Idaho a straight shot.

The massive man took one knee and bumped his cock head against the boy's pink box. Fred held the tip and shoved it inside. Idaho was astonished at how easily the head went in. He leaned forward, forcing more of his gigantic meat inside the kid's shitter. The boy let out a cry of pain.

Idaho tried to pull back, but the boy held his cock firmly and forced more and more inside his hole.

"Go all the way, man; I can take it."

Idaho shrugged. Fuck it. The kid would scream, and it would all be over. He walked forward on his knees, pushing inch after inch into the bottomless hole.

Fred shrieked like a schoolgirl. "Yes! Yes! Keep going! Deeper!"

Idaho was halfway in, much further than he usually got. He was glad he'd showered at the public pool that morning. There, he got a lot of stares but no takers. Now, he was halfway to paradise.

"Is it all the way in?"

"Nope. I got another six or seven inches to go."

"Oh fuck, Idaho, you're so fucking huge. You're making me wet."

Idaho glanced down at the boy's tiny, shriveled penis. Sure enough, it was dripping with semen, forced out by the pressure of his thick cock against the prostate. This made him even harder. He had reached the end of the kid's poop chute. He felt pressure build as he pressed against the back wall.

Then, the kid did something amazing. He twisted to one side, and suddenly his cock popped through an opening. It made an audible 'pop!' as it broke through. At first, Idaho thought he might have torn the poor boy open.

"What happened? Are you okay?"

Fred laughed. He lifted his head and turned back to stare at Idaho. "You popped through the second hole. Go for it! I'm all yours."

Idaho nearly cried for joy as he slid another four inches of flesh into the boy. When he realized there was no resistance, he went the whole way. Just as his hips touched the boy's ass cheeks, his cock bumped into another wall.

"Yes! That's it! You got to the second wall! Keep pushing!"

Idaho only had an inch or two left. The boy spread his cheeks far apart, allowing the older man to bury himself to the hilt. His rough pubic hairs tickled the boy's butt. He withdrew a couple of inches and slammed in hard.

"Harder! Don't hold back! I need it, man!"

Idaho lifted the boy by his stomach to allow him to fuck in and out hard and fast. To his surprise, he could feel his cock as it slithered up the boy's hole.

"Watch this." Fred grabbed Idaho's shoulder and rotated until he was facing his lover. Now Idaho could see the outline of his cock as it forced its way to places most men never knew existed. The kid had talent.

To his surprise, Fred lifted himself until their lips met. They kissed passionately as Idaho pounded away. He took shallow strokes at first, but when the kisses grew more intense, he increased the length of his stroke, popping out of the second hole and back in. Each time, he heard that popping noise that sounded a little like someone smacking a bare butt.

Idaho let a few tears of joy escape. They traveled down his face, joining the kiss as a salty surprise.

Fred looked at Idaho. "Why are you crying?"

"You've made me so happy!"

The kid grinned. "Fucking is the best. Everybody wins!" Idaho noticed how his stubble had reddened the boy's mouth to match his apple cheeks. He also felt his hairy tummy growing wet from the boy's pre-cum. The tiny penis was hard now. It felt like a thumb as it pressed up against him.

Idaho closed his eyes and started fucking the way he had always wanted to but never could until now. When he opened his eyes, sweat pouring down his face, he saw the boy's eyes glazed over with ecstasy. The kid's mouth moved, but no words came out. Idaho needed to stop worrying about him. It was time for him to be selfish. His powerful hips rocked back and forth like a locomotive. The length of his strokes brought his cock head all the way to the boy's asshole and then all the way to the second wall in less than a second. It was far too powerful for a normal person. Fred wasn't normal.

"You okay?" He thought he should ask.

The kid made the OK symbol with his thumb and forefinger. His head lolled from side to side in time with the rocking of the caboose.

Idaho was close. He could feel his cock leaving slippery trails of precum in Fred's ass. His balls churned as though they were a living creature. They pulled up tightly against Fred's cock, preparing for the upcoming parade of semen.

"You ready, son?"

Fred nodded. "Yes, Daddy."

That word was just too much for Idaho. "Oh fuck! I'm gonna come!"

"Yeah?"

"Yeah, I'm gonna come."

Fred said, "Me too."

And without touching himself, the boy shot a massive load from his tiny dick, hitting Idaho on the chin and covering his face and the floor behind him with the sticky mess.

"Unhhh!" Idaho was beyond words now. He erupted, spewing molten lava deep inside the boy. After eight squirts, he was still going. All told, he shot thirteen times during this one orgasm.

The kid leaned back. His smile was a reward. Idaho had never finished up a fuck with a smiling partner. They usually made horrible grimaces and looked away. And these were women who could only take half of him. They didn't have another hole for him to fuck deeper. This boy did.

Idaho was about to pull away. The boy grabbed his arm.

"Don't. Stay inside me. Let's do it again."

The words were an aphrodisiac. His spent cock sprang to life again, buried inside the boy. The kid reached up and rubbed Idaho's furry chest, tracing circles around the nipples before he pinched both of them very hard. Nobody had ever done that to Idaho before. He was startled by how much it turned him on.

"Keep doing that while I fuck you."

"Yes, Daddy."

There it was again. That word. He jackrabbited in and out in shallow strokes until he was fully hard, then switched to longer strokes. Pop! The cock pushed in and out of the second hole. The boy was nearly torturing his tits. But it was the least he could do to let him since he was giving him such a merciless fucking. With one hand on Idaho's nipple, Fred reached around and put a wet finger against the man's hole. He wormed his finger inside. It was painful, but Idaho allowed it. He never understood how any guy could stand to be fucked. But Fred loved it. Between the nipple and the finger, he was hurting a little. Then Fred pressed against his prostate. Idaho's mind was blown. He spread more precum throughout the kid's guts. It came in buckets.

"Shit! That feels so good."

Fred nodded. "I know. How about now?"

Fred snuck a second finger in, allowing him to press even harder while he stretched Idaho's hole. Idaho was a confident man. But this boy had him doubting his masculinity. He had never let anyone inside him like that. It was like being a woman. But it felt good. With each additional finger, Idaho felt his inhibitions lift. He wanted the boy to penetrate him. His little cock wouldn't be able to, but his hand sure could. He gasped when the thumb joined its fingers inside him. Fred pushed his Vaseline-coated fist into Idaho. Each time Idaho drew back, he got a fistful of fingers. Fred was persistent and talented. Once his hand popped in, he didn't let it out. He just let each stroke Idaho took help him bury his fist deeper inside the man.

Pretty soon, it was Fred who was doing all the fucking. Idaho stayed buried deep inside the boy, who at the same time was buried up to the forearm. The older man could feel the pretty boy push his fist through the second hole. He heard the same popping noise he heard earlier.

Fred fucked Idaho hard with his arm, popping in and out of the second hole with abandon. Idaho was still rock hard and close to coming again. The pressure at his prostate was pushing out a lot of clear, sticky liquid. When Fred got to the elbow, Idaho had an orgasm. It wasn't his cock. He was quivering hard inside. His ass was coming. He writhed upon the boy's arm, feeling his fingers tickling his guts somewhere deep inside.

"Oh, fuck man! Fuck!"

Fred punched hard, coming all the way out of Idaho's hole, then going elbow-deep. It was both excruciating and exquisite. The pain and the pleasure could not be separated. They became one. Suddenly, the older man's balls pulled up tight.

"I'm coming."

Fred nodded. He pulled his fist out of Idaho and leaned back, enjoying the hot sticky sensation as the cum pooled deep inside him. Idaho couldn't believe how hard and how much he came, even more than the first time. He felt a hot spray on his furry tummy and realized that Fred had come a second time as well, again without touching himself.

"How do you do that?"

Fred shrugged. "It's just one of my many talents."

Idaho looked Fred Talmadge in the eyes. "Will you do that again for me?"

"I was just going to ask you the same thing after bumming a cigarette."

The young hobo and his older companion rode the rails together. In the hobo jungles, they always found an out-of-the-way place to fuck and fist. The youth was father to the man in all things sexual. He showed him pleasures most of us only dream about.

One night, Idaho asked, "What do you want to do with your life?"

Fred answered, "I'm ambitious. I want to keep doing this forever."

DUMBO

Idaho had a good friend who rode along the Atchison, Topeka, and Santa Fe lines. His nickname was "Dumbo" because he had a cock that hung down like a baby elephant trunk. The two had commiserated over the impossibility of finding anyone. For a while, they had a convenient friendship: they jacked each other off. It was hard work, but it was easier than jacking themselves off. The touch of someone else's hand slicked up with spit, with eyes closed, was a turn-on. Kissing made it feel like sex.

One day in the Kansas City rail yards, Idaho and Fred bumped into Dumbo. He would know those smoldering green eyes and chiseled jaw anywhere.

"Idaho! How the fuck you been?"

"Good, Dumbo. Real good." He motioned with his eyes to his lover. "This here's Fred."

"Fred, Fred Talmadge, sir." The boy shook the handsome man's hand. It was a beautiful hand worthy of a Dorothea Lange photograph. It told a hundred stories in its cracks and crevices.

"Dumbo. Dumbo Colman." His eyes lingered on

the pretty boy's red lips. In a dress, he could pass as a girl. "So how do you know a sonofabitch like Idaho?"

Fred blushed. "He, uh. He's— "

Idaho cut in. "We're running buddies. We look out for each other."

Dumbo frowned. "How does a dainty fellow like Fred here look out for you?"

Fred and Idaho exchanged glances. Fred nodded.

"Well, Fred here is the only guy in the lower 48 who can take me."

Dumbo's jaw dropped. "That's impossible. You're even bigger than me."

Idaho shrugged. "Miracles can happen."

Dumbo frowned. "Does this mean we're not gonna 'take care of each other' like we used to?"

Idaho knew Fred would do anything he told him to do. He was supposed to protect the young man, but he also wanted to do Dumbo a favor. "I'm sure we can work something out."

FRED AND DUMBO

Fred knew what was in Idaho's mind. He was satisfied beyond all reason with his lover's monstrous cock nearly splitting him open every night. But he was ambitious. He always wanted something more. Fred knew he might miss an opportunity if he didn't speak up.

"Why do they call you Dumbo?"

The man didn't say anything, just dropped his dungarees, exposing an elephantine cock that wasn't nearly as thick as Idaho's, but it was definitely longer. It dangled to his knee half-hard.

Fred swallowed and looked at his lover. "Idaho, if you want to let Dumbo fuck me, I wouldn't mind."

Idaho smiled. "I think you'll enjoy it." He dug into his knapsack and gave the Vaseline to Fred.

Fred studied his lover to see if there were traces of jealousy in his smile. No, it was different. Idaho and Dumbo had once belonged to each other. It had been a deeper love than just sex. They had been companions. Idaho just wanted to share his good fortune. That's what the smile said.

The boxcar was half full of hay, which made for a

comfortable ride. Fred put Dumbo's cock in his mouth because he could. He went down until the head popped past his tonsils and rubbed his larynx. He looked over at Idaho, who had his big cock out, stroking it with two hands.

"Wish you could do that with me."

Fred shrugged. He couldn't talk with Dumbo's trunk blocking his windpipe. The long cock was growing a little thicker, probably from the excitement of having a mouth to fuck. Fred came up fast, spitting in his hand and rubbing it on his asshole. Dumbo turned him around and stuck his tongue in the boy's hole.

When he took a break, he said, "Your Uncle Dumbo's gonna fuck you from here to next Christmas. You want that?"

Idaho never did this. Idaho was good, but Dumbo was introducing him to a new kind of pleasure. Fred's eyes rolled back in his head.

"I want it. I want it bad."

Dumbo took a glob of Vaseline and wiped his cock with it before putting his greasy fingers into Fred's sopping wet hole. They slipped in like two prairie dogs returning to their burrow.

"Damn, Idaho. You tore this kid up. His ass is wider than a pussy."

Idaho grinned. "You'll thank me in a little while."

Fred wiggled his ass. He wanted Dumbo inside him real bad. Dumbo took two steps away from the little haystack over which Fred was slumped.

"You ready, boy?"

Fred nodded. His tiny cock was already dribbling with anticipation. "Fuck me, sir."

Dumbo was hesitant, just like Idaho had been.

Fred wanted all of the man inside him. He was thick, but Idaho was thicker. Fred surprised Dumbo when he guided his long cock through the second hole.

Dumbo hesitated. "Keep going?"

Fred had to stifle a sigh. "Fuck me all the way, Uncle."

The handsome green-eyed drifter rammed his cock all the way inside. He began to take long strokes that tickled. Fred had become so used to having a cock like a tin of beans that this beer can cock landed like a feather. The tickling caused Fred to spasm. His insides went insane. Until this moment, Fred hadn't ever experienced an anal orgasm like Idaho had done. Dumbo was an artist.

Fred's eyes turned white. His body bucked and jerked. His innards clamped down on and let go of the invading cock over and over. Fred had felt this on his arm when Idaho had an ass orgasm, so he knew what Dumbo was experiencing when the handsome hobo said, "Holy shit!"

In ecstasy, Fred only managed to say, "Oh, that's it," over and over. He caught Idaho's eye. The two had gotten very intimate in the previous months. They could read each other's minds. Fred jerked his head, inviting Idaho to join in the fun.

Fred pushed Dumbo on his back, riding him like a cowboy but facing away from him. He leaned back, lifting his legs, giving Idaho a passageway to paradise. The hulking drifter heaved his rock-hard monster skyward, letting it fall on Fred's tiny crotch. Fred cried out. Even little balls can hurt big.

Idaho pulled back and inserted the tip, feeling Dumbo's thrusts against his cock head.

Idaho looked into Fred's eyes. "Are you sure?"

Fred nodded. "Fuck me, Daddy. I need it all." Then Fred felt the worst pain since his first sexual experience, which was more rape than sex. But this was different. Fred invited Idaho in. He knew it would hurt, and he knew he would get used to it. With each additional inch from Idaho, the pain worsened. Maybe he was wrong. Maybe it wouldn't get better. But it did.

PLUGGING THE HOLE

The two old friends bumped balls while they shared the boy's hole. The rubbing and friction varied out of phase with their thrusts, making Idaho shudder. Dumbo moaned from below. Hearing his old flame made Idaho horny. He sped up his thrusts, caressing Fred's chest. Fred's eyes went glassy. Idaho worried he might be doing damage.

"Does it hurt?"

Fred shook his head. "Not anymore." Then, his eyes glazed over again. Idaho knew not to interrupt the kid in a fugue state.

Idaho grunted. Dumbo grunted louder. The two friends growled and snarled in short bursts. Fred whined and bleated.

The older men's cocks were intertwined inside the boy, so they had to move together as one. Idaho could feel Dumbo's cock pulsing in time with him. It was the closest the two old friends had ever been. Idaho kissed Fred, then leaned to the right and kissed Dumbo. He remembered the taste of his mouth and the shape of his long tongue. They stayed that way for a long time. Then Idaho straightened up and kissed his young lover, who was more like a son than a comrade. Fred twisted Idaho's nipples. It was a signal that he wanted him to come.

Idaho tapped Dumbo on the leg. The green-eyed traveler understood it was time. They picked up the pace, creating a flesh jackhammer boring its way through Fred's guts. Fred leaned back, resting his back against Dumbo's furry chest. He turned and kissed him. Idaho joined in; they were in a three-way lip lock.

It began to rain. Idaho looked up and got an eyeful of Fred's cum. The boy had tiny balls, but they could churn out more cum than Idaho. When Dumbo realized he was being showered with hands-free boy cum, he lost control.

"Fuck, I'm coming!" Dumbo twitched and jerked.

The movements sent Idaho over the edge. "Me too. Me too."

And in perfect sync, the two old friends unloaded their balls into the young man.

"Shoot inside me, Daddy. Fill me up, Uncle Dumbo."

Idaho went to that place where guys go when they come. The world melted around him until he was the only one there. He held Fred's tiny hand with his big mitts, anchoring him to Earth.

Dumbo was longer than Idaho, so his cum was further up the colon. Idaho coated his friend's cock head with his shooting cum. What goes up must come down. Idaho felt his own cum flowing back to him. Then he felt Dumbo's cum coat his cock head and squeeze its way into any possible crevice left in the stuffed sausage that was his lover. When the two friends pulled out, a rivulet of cum gushed out of the boy's stretched hole. They laughed when they saw how Dumbo's cock had wrapped around Idaho's like a two-strand braid. It took them a moment to disentangle their cocks. Fred was on his back in the hay, adding a little white gravy to some horse's meal. His ass was open so wide Idaho could see the lining of his rectum. It was bright red. The dark flaps of skin on either side of his hole looked like pussy lips.

"You ain't gonna hear your farts for a month," said Dumbo.

The three men agreed on an itinerary to get them to the town of Santa Fe, which had the finest hobo jungle west of the Mississippi. They slept in the hay, exhausted from sex.

BREAKFAST

At dawn, the train crept through East Colorado. Fred slept with his hand on Idaho's heart and his head on Dumbo's chest. The two men awoke before Fred. They brewed some coffee on Dumbo's camp stove and then made scrambled eggs.

"Fred, the eggs are getting cold."

The kid was passed out. He'd really taken a beating the day before. He wouldn't wake up for a few more hours. Idaho had good news.

"Dumbo, I've been practicing with Fred. I think I can take you."

Dumbo wore a puzzled expression. "But— "he gestured towards Fred's little penis.

Idaho clenched his fingers and held up a fist. A light went on in his friend's noggin.

"Idaho, do you honestly think you can take it?"

"Only one way to find out."

The little haystack was occupied with the sleeping beauty. Dumbo pulled down an unopened bale. Idaho lay with his back flat, lifting his legs in the air. He handed the tub of Vaseline to Dumbo, who took care of business. The green-eyed hobo spit in his palm and gave his semi-hard cock a few tugs until it was slick. He didn't know it, but he had the kind of cock that is made for fucking ass if it were a normal size. The head was smaller than the shaft, which turned his hardon into a missile. The over-long cock was thicker in the middle and tapered as it disappeared into the pubic bush. This meant that once he passed the middle, Idaho's ass would pull him in deeper as the butthole tightened.

Dumbo spat in his hand and wiped it on Idaho's greased-up ass. He put a couple of fingers in, surprised by how loose and elastic his friend was.

"Fred did this?"

Idaho nodded.

"Can he do it for me?"

Idaho said, "I don't see why not. But first things first. Fuck me."

Dumbo took a few steps back to position his head at the hole. He went slow until he realized that Idaho wasn't giving any kind of resistance. He shrugged, then walked forward, watching his lengthy cock disappear inside his friend's ass. The feeling of rubbing up against the second hole and then popping through was exquisite. He was glad that Idaho had found a young lover, but he still carried a flame for his old jack-off buddy. When he was buried to the hilt, he smacked Idaho's ass.

"Shit, Idaho, you're so loose it's like throwing a hot dog down a hallway."

Idaho smiled. "I kinda overdid it these past few months. You can fuck me hard, and it won't hurt."

Dumbo had a long journey to pull back and push back in. He started with little dog humps and progressed to locomotive-style pounding. His cock head was small, so it didn't make the popping sound, but the middle of his thick cock did if he fucked fast enough. Idaho pulled his friend close. He kissed him, looking straight into his eyes.

Idaho said, "I love you, old friend."

Dumbo smiled. "I know."

While Fred slept, the two men fucked with abandon. Dumbo had never fucked ass until the day before, so he was still learning the ropes. When he had been tangled up inside Fred, sliding alongside Idaho's fat cock, he discovered a few basic techniques. But Dumbo's dick was different, and he needed to find his own moves. When he pulled back further than anticipated, the fat center of his cock passed through the second hole, making a little popping sound.

Idaho said, "Yes! Right there! Oh, Jesus, right there! Do it again! Again!"

Dumbo looked over, but Fred was still sound asleep. "You like that, huh?"

"Yes. Oh God, Oh Jesus. Keep doing it like that." Idaho's innards made the popping sound over and over. With each stroke, Idaho's cock grew harder. It lifted off his leg and reached skyward. Soon, it was straight overhead. It was then that Idaho lost the power of speech and slowly moaned.

Seeing his friend so satisfied was a huge turn-on. Dumbo was a lonely guy, and Idaho had been his one friend who could commiserate about the burden of carrying a huge cock. He marveled at Idaho's towering cock in the daylight. All their jackoff sessions had been at night. It was magnificent, uncircumcised, with blue veins crawling skyward from the base. The head was so big, he wondered how Fred could take it. Dumbo wanted to learn how to get fucked by that fat pole. He licked it while he sent his friend into paroxysms of pleasure. Idaho thrashed on the hay bale, pounding his fists against the sides.

"You're gonna make me—" Idaho didn't finish his sentence.

Dumbo had visited Yellowstone and seen Old Faithful. Idaho's cock was more awe-inspiring. Dumbo watched in fascination as his friend churned out blast after blast of white cum. It rained down on the two men. They both needed a good hot shower.

The spectacle was an aphrodisiac. So used to using his hands, Dumbo didn't realize he was so close. Suddenly, his balls pulled up tight.

"Idaho, I'm coming."

"Come in me. I want you to come inside me." The husky hobo flexed his pec muscles and brought his arms around his old friend.

And all at once, the walls of the boxcar fell away, and Dumbo flew straight to the clouds. When it was over, he landed hard back in his body. Even Idaho noticed.

"Hey, where did you go?"

Dumbo didn't answer. He kissed his friend's nipples, cheek, mouth. Between them was a log of flesh still throbbing from earlier. The head touched Idaho's chin. Dumbo put his mouth over the tip, licking it.

"Stop, you'll get me hard again."

Fred stood with his hands on his hips, smiling broadly. "I hope you do. It's my turn."

STRETCHING LESSONS

Fred gave lessons to his lover's ex-lover. He wasn't mad or jealous. He had never been happier when they were both inside him. To make sure it happened every night, he needed to give Dumbo a reason to stay. Once Dumbo tried Idaho's cock, the three would become one. Dumbo would never leave. Fred loved getting fucked by Idaho's enormous cock, and Dumbo would too.

The first lesson didn't go well. Dumbo cried "Uncle" at three fingers. Fred didn't think it was bad for his first day, but Dumbo moped around the boxcar as the train rushed down the Western Rockies.

"Hey, don't be sad. You did well."

Dumbo said, "You're just saying that."

Fred rubbed the handsome hobo's shoulders. "Relax. Relax. Relax. That's the key."

Dumbo said, "I wish there were a magic pill that would make me relax."

Fred laughed. "You want a Quaalude next time? That will help. Quaaludes are prescribed for anxiety and sleep, but they make a fantastic muscle relaxer, too."

The next night after supper, Fred gave Dumbo a Quaalude. Fred knew the hobo was suspicious of all medicines, but he had said he wanted a "magic pill." Dumbo washed it down with canteen water.

Fifteen minutes went by. Dumbo said, "I don't feel anything."

Fred smiled. "Give it a chance."

Another ten minutes went by. Dumbo's eyes widened. "I feel something."

Fred said, "You're gonna feel a lot more in a few minutes."

Soon, numbness and euphoria clouded Dumbo's mind.

Fred needed to break Dumbo, get him to open up. Dumbo grinned at the boy. "Let's give this a go, kid."

Fred greased up his fingers and smeared a thick coat of Vaseline on Dumbo's butt hole. He decided to start with two fingers, then worked his way up to three.

"How's that feeling?"

Dumbo exhaled loudly. "It doesn't hurt as much. Go for four."

Fred obliged. He slid in and out of the greasy hole as deep as his open thumb would allow. Then he folded the thumb and punched his way in.

"Owww! Shit!" Dumbo was on the verge of tears.

Fred said, "Wait 30 seconds; I promise it will go away."

Dumbo pounded the hay bale. "Oh, fuck it hurts! It hurts. Oh, it doesn't hurt anymore."

Fred pressed forward, causing Dumbo's big dick to leak a thin stream of pre-cum. Then Fred retreated, letting his fist get caught in the tight hole, pulling on it but not exiting.

"Does that hurt, sir?"

Dumbo chuckled. "It doesn't. This pill is a fucking miracle!"

Fred let his instincts and the contours of Dumbo's insides dictate his movements. The handsome hobo heaved a sigh of pure pleasure. That was Fred's cue to move into the next phase. He bunched up his fingers and pushed through to the colon. It made a satisfying pop. Dumbo's thighs shook.

"Damn! I never knew how good it would feel."

Fred nodded. "Wait until you let Idaho fuck you."

The young hobo pushed more and more of his arm into the man, stretching the tight hole like a rubber band. Dumbo relaxed and let Fred punch his guts for an hour. His cock finally got hard, pressed tightly to his belly and chin. He stroked himself. Fred used his free hand to help out. There was so much dick to stroke; between them, they couldn't cover it all. Dumbo howled like a coyote. His shallow breath came in short bursts. His face was relaxed. He was in the zone.

"Fred, I'm gonna come."

"Wait." The young man changed angles so he could take Dumbo's cock in his mouth. He let the head slide past his tonsils.

"I'm coming!"

Fred felt the hot burst of cum shoot down his throat. Holding his breath, he forced the spurting cock deep in his throat. He didn't need to swallow. The cum was already on its way to his stomach. Dumbo came for almost a minute. When the last trickle was released, Fred pulled his head back and let the spent cock hit his face.

Idaho whistled. "Goddamn, that was hot. I'd join you in a second round, but we gotta hop off. We're just outside Santa Fe."

HOBO JUNGLE

The hobo jungle in Santa Fe was a country club compared to Chicago or St. Louis. Just outside of town, the encampment had once been the office and changing room of a defunct coal mine. The office was massive, a crazy quilt of free crash pads. The changing room had hot and cold running water and open showers. After claiming a campsite, the friends made a beeline for the showers to wash three days of sex and diesel dust off their bodies.

The trio made quite the picture in the showers. Without giving it much thought, they chose three consecutive shower heads, with Fred in the middle. A toothless bum did his best to whistle.

"Jesus Christ on a cross. Would you look at that?"

The room of men swiveled their heads to look at the three.

The toothless one continued. "It's like a rabbit caught between two horses!"

The whole shower room erupted in laughter except for the three friends. Fred stood defiantly and glared. Idaho put a protective arm around him. It was hard to understand, but Idaho was easily shamed about his own size. He was partly holding on to Fred to calm his own nerves. Dumbo didn't give a shit. When the room quieted down, he laughed back at the crowd.

"We got more dick here between the three of us than all y'all combined. And that's counting the little one!"

It was a tense moment, but then the other men laughed and nodded. One of them said, "You got a point there."

Another hobo chimed in. "A really, really big point." More laughter.

Idaho was concerned for Fred. It hurts to be humiliated for your size, but the little guys were less able to laugh it off. He thought he saw tears form in the corners of his baby-faced boyfriend's eyes, but it might have just been the shower water.

He whispered. "Don't let them get to you, Fred. You have a beautiful, fuckable body. Be proud of who you are."

The toothless old man who started the confrontation came over and introduced himself. "Joe Hilliard. Welcome to Camp Santa Fe." His hand was extended towards Fred. The boy shook the old man's hand. Idaho noticed the old man was hung small like Fred. Maybe smaller.

Joe said, "I got a bottomless mouth and no teeth. You two come find me if you need a change from this handsome little man."

Fred cleared his throat. "You gotta ask me for permission. These are my guys, and I don't loan them out to just anyone."

Idaho was stunned. Fred was small, but he had a

dominant personality. He was tempted by the offer from the man with no teeth. If anybody could suck his cock, it would be this old fart. He could just close his eyes and pretend it was a young, handsome boy. If Fred allowed it.

"Fred, I've never gotten a blow job. You know this might be my only chance."

Fred nodded. "Joe, you think you can handle Idaho here?"

The old man held his chin between thumb and forefinger. "I dunno. I was thinking about this guy," gesturing towards Dumbo. He shook his head and said, "Idaho is awful thick."

Idaho felt his heart sink. God had blessed him so hard it turned into a curse.

Joe caught Idaho's eye. "Still, I can always try."

After dressing, Idaho went to Joe's tent. The space was kept very tidy. The old man had a comfortable, clean mattress. Idaho lay down on it and sighed. Hay is soft but not like an Airflex mattress.

Joe stretched his jaw with his hands. With no teeth to hold onto, he just put one fist in his mouth and tried to get in a few fingers more. He pulled his fist and three fingers out of his mouth and held it over the tip of Idaho's swelling cock. It was bigger, but it might not be soon.

"I'm gonna try. I got no tonsils and no teeth. I don't gag, neither."

This was new to Idaho, who had never once gotten this far along with a blow job.

Quickly, the old man put the semi-hard head into his mouth and used gravity to force it past the uvula. Idaho wasn't sure what would happen if the monster reached full size. He'd let Joe worry about it. He lay back and let the man bob up and down until it became lodged in his airway.

Joe couldn't speak, so he tapped then pounded on Idaho's thigh. Idaho lifted himself onto his elbows and saw the emergency unfolding. It made his erection fade. Like magic, Joe pulled himself off the colossal cock and sat on his haunches, gasping for air.

Idaho shrugged. "It was worth a try." He reached for his pants.

"Now hang on." Joe waggled a finger at him. "Patience pays."

To his surprise, Idaho watched as the man held a deep breath, then swallowed inch after inch of cock. He got halfway. Idaho could see the outline of his cock pressing against Joe's esophagus.

"Holy cow. I never imagined— "Idaho drifted off because the old man was humming. The vibrations were unlike anything Idaho had ever experienced with women or with Fred. "Oh shit. That feels so good." Seeing the outline of his cock in the man's throat was such a turn-on that he didn't even close his eyes.

Joe's face was bright red. When his ears turned blue, he pulled off Idaho's cock and took several deep breaths.

"Son, you got a huge fucking dick. This may take a while."

When Idaho had lost a little of the swell, Joe went down again, this time even farther. He bobbed his head rapidly in small movements. Idaho watched in fascination as his huge cock head moved past the Adam's apple. Once it did, Joe took in a few more inches. Idaho was in disbelief. It seemed impossible from a scientific viewpoint. Maybe Joe was deformed.

Thinking about the blow job in such a clinical manner caused Idaho to soften. Joe wasted no time, burying his face in Idaho's pubic bush. There, he bobbed up and down for as long as he could take it, then pulled back all the way, letting Idaho's cock flop onto his thigh.

"Man, you're amazing." Idaho realized he had tears in his eyes. He felt a 30-year curse just lifted. "You don't have to finish."

Joe frowned. "The fuck I don't. Hold still." The old man swallowed Idaho's entire manhood in a single motion, his nose touching the pubic mound. He pulled all the way out and took a breath, then back down, over and over. Now Idaho knew what he'd been missing.

"Oh, shit, that feels good. Oh god. Keep doing that."

And Joe kept doing it. It took ten minutes before Idaho felt the slick drops of clear semen bubbling out the tip.

"I'm close."

Joe nodded. He had his little penis out, jerking it hard and fast. Idaho marveled at nature's extremes for a split second before succumbing to the first wave of pleasure. An orgasm was imminent. Idaho's body jerked involuntarily.

Joe knew about orgasms. Taking a giant breath, he forced the fat cock all the way down his throat until his face pressed hard against Idaho's crotch. Then, he made tiny, rapid bobbing motions.

Idaho erupted. He pumped ounce after ounce of cum down the old guy's throat. Joe pulled back slowly, squeezing Idaho's cock past the larynx. Idaho's monster fell from Joe's mouth, still spraying cum everywhere. Joe pointed it at his face and let Idaho do his clown makeup. He was a soggy, toothless mess. He stuck out his tongue and caught droplets of Idaho's semen like snowflakes.

Idaho thanked Joe and returned to the camp. He didn't need a shower. He hadn't broken a sweat, and the old man had graciously cleaned his pecker.

When Idaho got back to the tent, Dumbo was cumming deep inside Fred. He shouted as the youngster whined and moaned.

"Goddammit, yes! Yes!" Dumbo collapsed on the boy's back, out of breath.

Fred saw Idaho and smiled. "How did he do?"

Idaho said, "I'm going to give you so much candy and amphetamine that your teeth fall out. Is that cool?"

DINNERTIME

At dinner around the campfire, Joe was quiet. When someone asked him a question, he spoke in a hoarse whisper. Idaho knew he was responsible. Before he could worry, Joe looked at him and winked. It was no problem.

Back at the tent, the three made a bed out of open sleeping bags. It was warm out, so they didn't need a blanket.

Dumbo stripped naked. "I can't deal with pajamas."

Fred and Idaho followed suit.

Fred put Dumbo's soft cock in his mouth and worked on it. Idaho greased up Fred, preparing to be the meat in the man sandwich. But Dumbo surprised him.

"Why don't you lay behind me? I'm ready to let you fuck me."

Idaho hadn't prepared mentally to be the man on top. But he watched as Fred put Dumbo's slippery cock into his ass and took the whole length inside in one smooth motion. The only hole left was Dumbo's.

"Are you sure, man? I don't want to hurt you."

Dumbo said, "You got to hurt me to fuck me. The pain won't last."

Fred lay on his side. He rode Dumbo like a ride at Disneyland.

Dumbo didn't move. He let Fred do all the work.

Idaho watched his old friend and his new friend fucking. It aroused him. His limp cock expanded and lengthened until he was at full erection. Dumbo's asshole was already lubricated. He and Fred had planned this, no doubt.

Idaho took a finger full of Vaseline and coated his cock until it shone like a chrome bumper. Carefully, he put the first third of his cock head inside his well-hung friend.

Dumbo seemed focused on his intense fuck with Fred. He didn't protest. To Idaho's amazement, Dumbo didn't resist when he pushed it halfway in. There was some definite panic when it reached the Corona. Idaho pushed quickly, and his cock popped inside.

"Fuck that feels better than a fist, for sure." Dumbo was high. He had already taken a Quaalude and was now taking sniffs of modeling glue to distract his brain. "Don't hold back, Idaho, fuck me like you mean it."

Idaho held his green-eyed friend by the hip to allow him to push in farther. It was moving as smoothly as a Pullman car. He didn't meet much resistance when he popped past the second hole. After that, it was a freeway to the finish line. Idaho's hips bumped into Dumbo's butt.

Dumbo howled with joy. "I did it! We did it!"

Idaho said, "It's just started. Let's get to the finish

line." The hulking hobo withdrew all but the tip and rammed it home.

"Oh fuck! Fuck! Keep doing it just like that. Just like that." Dumbo took another sniff of glue. His head drooped, and he relaxed even further. Idaho knew he could pound his old friend with abandon, so he did.

When Dumbo came out of his glue fog, he stared into Idaho's eyes. "This is all I've ever wanted." Neither man noticed that Fred had vanished.

Idaho was focused on the task at hand. He grunted in response. Dumbo was sexy as fuck, but he talked too much.

"Did you stop loving me when you left?"

"Shh! Quiet time." Idaho put a finger across Dumbo's ruby-red lips.

Dumbo shut up. Idaho kept his focus. He plumbed the depths of his old friend, intent and anxious to leave his seed inside him.

Fred must have given Dumbo some tips. The green-eyed hobo reached up and twisted Idaho's nipples. Now it was Idaho whose head was lolling back. This only encouraged Dumbo. He twisted harder and reached up to suck his nipples.

Dumbo's pretty lips on his chest kept Idaho in a deep reverie. His head flooded with memories of his old friend, their shared secret, the companionship, and those many nights jerking each other off.

Idaho looked into Dumbo's eyes. "I never stopped loving you, man."

These were magic words because Dumbo's cock, limp since Fred left, came to life under Idaho's belly. He watched in fascination as it went from very long to impossibly long. Dumbo didn't show until he was hard. When they first met, Dumbo told Idaho he got the nickname when he was completely soft. He said, "If they'd seen me hard, I would be called Babar now."

The reference was lost on Idaho then, but he later went to the public library in Joplin. He took a sink bath, then searched until he found the book in the kid's section. Babar wasn't a baby; he was fully grown—an Elephant King.

Idaho couldn't take his eyes off his friend's huge cock. Without a second thought, he scooped up Dumbo's trunk and filled his mouth.

"Oh shit, Idaho, that's too much. Stop. Don't. Stop."

Idaho smiled. "Okay, I won't stop." He sucked until he tasted the first salty drops that heralded an imminent ejaculation. Then he let the cock drop. He knew his friend wouldn't feel too great if Idaho had to fuck him for hours after he came.

He had brought Dumbo to the edge of a precipice, then pulled him back. A rivulet of clear sticky fluid dribbled from the throbbing cock. Teasing his friend, Idaho licked the precum off the head, making him almost come.

Dumbo shivered and shook his head. He put his hands firmly on Idaho's tits and pinched them hard a dozen times in rapid succession. Idaho felt the end of his cock leaking a little. It mixed with the Vaseline to form the perfect frictionless lube. The only place where Idaho's cock met with resistance was at the second hole and then again when pulling out completely. So, he adjusted his strokes to maximize contact with the two tight holes. He tried not to slip out all the way, but once in a while he did. Some air got trapped each time, building up inside. With his cock deep in his friend, he felt the air rush past and escape. A loud wet fart punctuated the moment. Idaho was a little ashamed of how much it turned him on. He kept pushing air and letting it escape. The vibrations sent shivers down his spine. The sound was disgusting and funny in equal measure. Idaho got hard, closing the gap as his flesh swelled to its maximum girth. Now, the air couldn't escape.

Dumbo said, "Pull out, buddy, I gotta fart again."

Idaho retreated, leaving a gaping hole where Dumbo's pink pucker had once been. There was no sound this time, just a breeze from within. As soon as the air escaped, Idaho shoved his cock back in. The slippery walls of his friend's guts resisted again. Idaho gave a hard thrust; he went until his pubes tickled Dumbo's ass. He stayed there, taking small strokes and bumping over and over again into the last wall. Then something new happened. As his strokes grew more intense, he felt his cock push upwards at the end. Idaho didn't know much about anatomy, so he didn't realize he had driven his cock into the descending colon.

Dumbo's teeth chattered. He shivered. His eyes rolled back in his head. Idaho saw it and was worried.

"Did I hurt you?"

"Nah, man. Keep doing it. Just like that."

The junction between colons was tight enough to tickle Idaho's humongous cock head. He kept going there over and over, probing into new territory. Not even Fred had reached this magic spot. A trail of saliva ran down Dumbo's cheek. He was in ecstasy. He leaned forward and clamped his mouth on Idaho's left tit, right over his heart. He felt the handsome hulk's heart beating against his cheek. Like a newborn, he nursed. He nibbled, bit sucked, and licked.

Idaho knew he was close when Dumbo found his right nipple and pinched it, then twisted it. He grunted like a farm animal.

"Are you ready?"

Dumbo nodded. Idaho pulled his friend's cock head to his mouth and swallowed as much as he could, which wasn't much. It was enough. Dumbo twisted and writhed with imminent orgasm. He churned out a salty load of the clear stuff. Idaho swallowed like it was whisky. Idaho thought about his dirty love of farts. He drew close to the edge by thinking about his cock as an air pump, creating farts inside his friend. Dumbo bit down hard on his tit. That was the final straw.

Their mouths full of each other, they said nothing. There was no warning, no timing. With a mighty thrust, Idaho tipped.

At the same time, Dumbo felt his friend's swirling tongue on his dick. It was too much.

They came together. Idaho flooded Dumbo's colon with his baby gravy. Dumbo returned the favor in Idaho's mouth while nursing his nipple. Idaho savored his friend's cum before swallowing it all.

Spent, the two collapsed into each other's arms. Idaho suddenly remembered Fred. He must have left when Idaho and his old buddy got too wrapped up in each other. He hoped Fred wasn't mad.

WHERE ANGELS TREAD

Dumbo succumbed to the Quaaludes and drifted off to a blissful sleep. Idaho shimmied into his dungarees and walked the camp looking for his little buddy. He spied Joe, who gave a toothless grin and waved him over.

"Hey, Idaho. Ready for round two?"

Idaho shook his head politely. "I'm looking for Fred. Have you seen him?"

Joe said, "Yeah. He's catching a boxcar to Los Angeles. Leaves in about five minutes."

Idaho ran towards the railyards a few blocks away. If he ran fast enough, he might catch Fred. Tears streamed down his face. He ran and ran. He heard the train whistle blow once. That was good. It meant they were stopping. It would be at least another five minutes until the train gave two long blasts and departed.

"Hey, which track goes to Los Angeles?" Idaho prayed this hobo was a local. His prayers were answered.

The man pointed. "Six tracks from this one."

"Thank you. Thank you." Idaho kissed the man

on his forehead and ran. He saw Fred in a boxcar with another man. Breathless, he reached the car.

"Fred! Fred!"

The curly-headed cherub leaned out of the car. Behind him, a short young hobo lay face down, his bare bottom pointed skyward.

The supine young man said, "Fred, hurry up!" His ass was enormous. "Get back here and fuck me. I can take it." Idaho puzzled over those words. Take what? Fred was tiny.

Fred said, "Idaho. Why are you here?"

"You're gonna fucking leave me?"

Fred nodded. I got ambitions, Idaho. Besides, my work with you is done. Time for me to go back to the city of angels."

"Your work?"

"You and Dumbo split because you couldn't satisfy each other. I showed you how. You love each other."

"But I love you, Fred!"

Fred chuckled. "Go back to your man. I taught you how to love and how to fuck. I've got another soul to work on now." He jerked his head towards the hungry bottom behind him.

Idaho noticed Fred was naked. His eyes grazed his crotch, looking for his beautiful, tiny penis. It wasn't there. A massive cock, the girth of Idaho's, hung between Fred's short legs, halfway to the floor.

"Who are you?"

"I'm whoever you need me to be."

The train gave two long blasts. The boxcar lurched forward slowly. Idaho ran beside the car.

"Fred, come back! We can make it work, the three of us."

"No, Idaho. You and Dumbo are in love. You know it's love because you loved me. I brought you back together. Now, let me get started on Dougie back here. He's ashamed of his big butt; I am gonna make him love it."

The train was building momentum. Idaho had to jog to keep up.

"But I love you, Fred!"

Fred smiled. "I know. Now go back to Dumbo and love some more."

That was the last thing Idaho heard from the young man who'd altered the course of his life. Fred was a magical creature in human form, but not human. Idaho knew in his heart that Dumbo was the true love of his life, not Fred. Nobody understood the miseries of a big dick like Dumbo did. And no human besides Dumbo could take his monster. Fred's carriage disappeared from view. Six tracks and five blocks gave him time to cry, curse, and accept that Fred was never his.

When Idaho walked into the tent, Dumbo was sound asleep. Idaho lay down beside him, spooning. Dumbo woke up. "Hey, man. Where's Fred?"

Idaho shook his head and kissed his man on the lips. "From now on, I'll be calling you Babar. King Babar if they ask."

THE TWO OLD FRIENDS EMBRACED, OVERWHELMED by the love that surrounded them.

"But seriously, where is Fred?" Dumbo sat up.

"He went back to the angels."

ON THE BLOCK

by J. W. Steed

The story that follows is not autobiographical, but in my youth, I was intimately familiar with its setting: a tiny area of downtown Richmond, Virginia, known to locals as the Block.

Starting with the Second World War, for four decades, the Block served as many things for many people: a social hub and nascent gay village for Richmond's LGBTQ community, a nighttime hotbed for male and trans sex workers and their mostly suburban customers, and an easy spot for the police department's vice squad to prey upon a population whose sexuality was, at the time, criminalized.

The HIV/AIDS crisis of the nineteen-eighties erased the Block's community and its unrecorded history. Today, the neighborhood could belong to any gentrified downtown. I intend my story to capture a moment shortly before the Block's extinction when the streets were a little seedier, the foot traffic more convivial, and the atmosphere much, much gayer—in every sense of the word.

LUCKY CHARM

"**S**uck it. Yeah. Suck it. Fuck yeah. Suck it."

The dude I'm blowing doesn't go for much variation in his dirty talk, that's for sure. Like a lot of men who cruise the Block after dark, he's one of those so-called straight guys with an office job, a comb-over, and a wedding ring. Saying aloud the words *suck it* is probably the most erotic thing he's done in months. But he's taking his sweet time to shoot, and that's a problem. I've wasted the last several minutes on my knees in the tiny basement men's room of the downtown public library, trying to get him off with my hands and mouth and sheer willpower.

Those heavy balls aren't budging, though. In fact, about five minutes ago, I'd attempted to stumble to my feet and cut my losses. Then he'd fished out a ten-dollar bill from his poly blend slacks and shoved it into the front pocket of my new leather jacket, where it joined the twenty he'd given me earlier. It's enough incentive to keep going for a little bit more, sure. But there are only so many hours in the night, and my rent's due tomorrow.

Normally, I'd be all set, but this afternoon I spied this leather number in a Grace Street thrift shop and decided it's what I need to complete my street look. Matches my boots, too. Thanks to that impulse purchase, I'm a few bucks short and can feel the minutes ticking away. I need this john to finish up so I can move on to the next.

He guides my mouth away from his dick and tilts my chin upward. I'm hoping he'll beat himself off on my face, but instead, he bends down and whispers, "Kiss me, baby."

I shake my head. "No kissing." It's the one thing I won't do. He sighs, disappointed. I get back to work.

That's when I see it. Over by the exit, half tucked away beneath a battered waste can, I spy a shiny Kennedy half-dollar, face up. Maybe not so shiny. But it glints enough to catch my eye. I don't really believe in omens, but I know a good one when I see it.

I know—I've got thirty bucks in my jacket pocket. Compared to that, what's a random filthy coin? But see, that fifty cents is free money. A guy can do a lot with a half dollar. Fifty cents buys four songs on the jukebox or maybe even a happy hour beer down at Lum's. Fifty cents covers most of a bus fare or two games of Galaxian at the Station Break arcade. Fifty cents covers a tip for the barber, next time I go. Now that I've got that half dollar in my line of sight, all I can do is stare at it sideways, even while I deep-throat the guy's fat hog.

Time to break out some desperation tactics. There's one thing I've found that pushes most guys over the edge when they get head. Especially the buttoned-down married men for whom a same-sex blow job is their semi-annual walk on the wild wide. While I slide my lips over his fat six inches and tug at his balls with my right hand, I dig my left fingers into his tighty whities past his hairy taint and into the forbidden zone. Then I shove my left middle finger right in his warm pucker. He croaks out a protest that echoes around the little restroom once I dive in past the first knuckle.

When his balls tighten, I know it's all over. I've violated the one place straight men don't want touched, and despite himself, he loves it. Outrage is written all over his face, but he's so turned on at the line I've crossed that he instantly begins shooting. Sour semen jets against the back of my throat. I gulp and swallow it all down like a good boy.

Job done.

Once his dick skids out of my mouth, I maneuver out of the way so none of that goo messes up my new—used—leather. Then, in one graceful move, my fingers nick that half-dollar from under the trash and slide it into my tight jeans before I turn on the sink taps and wash the stink from my finger. Lucky find, that coin. It's definitely going to be a great night.

He's still zipping up in the stall, none the wiser. "What're you called?" he asks, tucking his shirt inside his briefs. "In case I want to see you again. So I can ask around."

What am I called? Sticky question. Guys on the Block use a nickname I hate, so I've been trying to toughen up my image. Thus, the jacket. "They call me Snake Eyes," I growl as I give my mouth a quick rinse and dry off with a paper towel.

The guy snorts with disbelief. "Snake Eyes?" I nod. "No, for real."

"Snake Eyes!"

"Son, my kid's Golden Retriever is more of a Snake Eyes than a big blond beefcake like you. Christ, you look like a Ken doll."

It's with a sigh that I concede. "Nick," I tell him. "Nicky. I'm around most nights."

"All right, kid." He chuckles to himself and fixes his pants. He's still shaking his head as he exits. "Snake Eyes!" I hear his laughter reverberating through the cavernous gloom outside the door.

❧

THE SUN'S BARELY GRAZING THE HORIZON BY THE time I finally emerge from the library, but the Block already buzzes with energy. There's a battle of the Summers already taking place: on the third story of one of the century-old townhouses, someone's opened wide their windows and Donna Summer is loudly feeling love. Further down Franklin, across the street, she's toot-tootin' and beep-beepin'. The clash is a disco mess, but it still gets my blood pumping, ready for whatever the next few hours will bring. Lucky night, remember?

Already, I'm getting appreciation for my new look. That's gratifying, considering how much I'd shelled out for the jacket. One of the other regulars, Al, a slightly older jock in all-white tennis gear, gives me a nod as we pass. Whatever type you dream of, you'll find it on the Block—jocks, preps, tough guys, femmes. Most don't tend to last too long. Richmond's a sleepy Southern burg that smart hustlers want to flee.

For me, it's a damned sight better than Galax,

where I grew up. This town is just a stepping stone to a bigger destination. Once I save up, I'll be moving up to D.C. or Philly. Maybe even the Big Apple. Someplace there's actual action. And johns with deeper pockets.

What we call the Block starts adjacent to the library—two blocks west on Franklin to the YMCA, a block south to Main, then back east again. During the daytime, it's a deserted and anonymous section of run-down townhouses in a part of the city where no nice folk want to live. After dinner, though, when those same nice folk are home with their families, the gays living in the apartments above play their music and hang out the windows, spectating. Some throw scarves over their table lamps to light their flats in pinks and blues. Others sit out on the steps to smoke cigarettes or joints and catch up on the day's gossip.

Then there's guys like me, who walk the Block.

Around and around I go, always on the outer ring of the two-block circuit, walking counterclockwise, down Franklin to Adams to Main and back to the library, lap after lap. Rent boys working the Block all tend to travel in the same direction, so we can see the faces of the potential johns slowly driving these one-way streets. They're prowling for guys like me who have something to sell. Cash only. Definitely no promissory notes. Sometimes, if they're single, I might end up with my backside in some stranger's bed across town, a fold of bills in my pocket, jeans on the floor. Since a lot of the johns are married, it's usually a hasty hand or blow job in their car, parked on some nearby side street.

Either way, I have rent due.

A beige Chevy Impala approaches, piloted by a round-faced little guy with equally round Mr. Peepers glasses. Curbside, I preen for him, chest puffed out, jacket open to show off the muscles under my tight tee, right thumb hooked in my jeans waistband, just above the fly. Maybe I do look like a big ol' Ken doll, but guys pay for that.

He's not buying, though. The driver sees something he likes better on the other side of the street, where a skinny Black man in short shorts and a cut-off shirt executes a clumsy spin on his roller skates. You can tell what flavor a john prefers by which lane of Franklin he drives. White hustlers occupy the outer sides; Black men tend to stay in the Block's inner ring. I don't know why. It's not a hard and fast rule. It's just the way it's done, and from what I've heard, it has always been that way.

Mr. Peepers has stopped his car. Over my shoulder, I see him speaking through the passenger window to the beanpole on skates. Timmy, I think his name is. Kimmy, maybe? I don't wait to see if they drive off. There'll be other cars and other johns. I wouldn't have minded a go at the bespectacled man. Sometimes those nerdy, timid types have the biggest cocks. Plus, they unload quickly.

I catch the eye of a thick-necked bulldog in a red pickup. A real blue-collar type. I get along fine with those guys. Hell, Galax was nothing but factory workers. Sometimes, though, they balk at my asking price. Rednecks are nowhere near as bad as bankers and big businessmen, though. Those guys can easily afford to drop bills on a cute piece of tail but still try to save a dime or two by haggling. Just last month, a rich asshole in a brand new '79 Corvette wanted to prorate my fee after he'd shot his wad in only five minutes. Fuck that. I know my worth.

My worth. Now I can't help but think of my poor mama, wearing one of her homemade floral house-coats, applying mercurochrome and tape to the marks on my face. *You've got to stay out of the way of those good old boys, Nicky. They don't understand the way you are. You're worth more than all of them put together. You'll see.* Her nickname for me had been Ferdinand, after a kid's story about a flower-sniffing bull. My dad just called me That Fucking Useless Dumb Ox.

Nope. Don't want to think about that.

I'd rather consider the hot piece perched on the steps of the Y, sticking out like a sore thumb. Fancy feathered auburn hair that's more red than brown. Blue eyes. Delicate features that don't make him any less masculine. The guy's good-looking, sure, but who wears slacks and a button-down on the Block? I give him the once-over while pretending to gauge the oncoming traffic. Expensive clothing that's not from a thrift store. A mustache nearly as thick as mine. Yeah, he's got a good facial hair game going on.

The guy stares my way without any inhibitions. I used to be an eager little pup, too, when I originally found the Block. I've learned since to play it cool. So I lean against the pillar, flanking the steps, and plant the flat of a foot against its bricks. From my jacket, I pull a pack of Fruit Stripe gum that I keep to freshen up my breath between tricks, unsheathe a stick of orange, and curl it into my mouth. When I look over my shoulder, he's still staring. Then he gives me a tentative smile.

It's obvious he's not going to make the first move. I nod, then gaze back at the street. Up above, someone else has added a third hi-fi to the cacophony, this one playing some new tune by the Electric Light Orchestra. I push myself up from the pillar and stroll past. Once I'm certain he's checking me out, I sit not beside him, but two steps up and a few feet away. If he wants to keep staring, he'll have to turn around.

Which he does. "You're a working boy."

His deep voice unglues my insides; it's so smooth and rich. Like butterscotch. That accent is definitely not from Virginia. He talks properly, without a drawl, like someone paid to be on TV. A weatherman or anchor. I don't fall for johns, but already I'm hoping this guy is that rare combination of cash up front plus fun in the sack. "Yup."

"For how long?"

I shrug. "Maybe three years."

The sight of his baby blues, crinkling at the edges when he grins in disbelief, melts me. Then, that Colgate smile. God damn. "Come on," he says. "You can't be any older than twenty-one."

I shrug again. I could be older than twenty-one. I'm not. But I could be. How old is he? I'm guessing late thirties. A thick gold wedding band adorns his finger. Of course.

He's swung around now to lay an arm across the top step, lounging to face me. I'm more than a little turned on. "It's pretty colorful at night here, huh?" He gestures to the townhouses opposite, where tenants have turned on more lights now that it's dusk. One window flashes with red and green Christmas lights.

"A regular fairyland for fairies." I'm pleased when my joke gets a deep and hearty laugh.

"You think of yourself as a fairy?" Weird question.

"Don't you?"

He chuckles. "I'm straight as an arrow, man."

He waggles his left fourth finger like it proves some kind of point. Time will tell on that one, *man*, I think to myself. How many guys wearing wedding rings have railed me in their station wagons and nice suburban sedans? Honestly, his answer would've been plain obnoxious if he hadn't said it with such a winning smile.

I sit up to adjust the lapels of my jacket. Already, my gum has lost its flavor, so I spit it into the foil. I'm about to suggest we get down to business when he adds, "Listen. I'm a reporter. I don't know if you've heard of *Newsweek*." Does the guy think I'm stupid? Everyone's heard of *Newsweek*. I take a gander at the card he pulls from his wallet to give me. Sure enough, it looks legit. *Winston Comstock III*, it says, with a New York address. There are a couple of phone numbers and something called a WATS line, too.

Everything falls into place once I read that snooty-sounding name. Years in an exclusive New England boarding school. An expensive college. Ivy League, probably. I can even hear the Yankee in his voice. "I'm doing a profile of places like the Block. Maybe you'd like to be its representative."

"Naw, I don't think..."

"You don't want some outsider judging you. Who knows? You might get a little fame out of it." The reporter reaches out to fish his card from my fingers. He tucks it into the top pocket of my jacket, where it joins the bills I've already collected for the evening. "Let me shadow you for a couple of nights. I mean, follow you around."

"I know what shadow means." I hate to admit it, but I'm tempted. Exposure might give me a leg up, help me relocate to a bigger and better city. It's pretty plain this northerner doesn't think much of my intellect, but I'm smart enough to know flirtation when I see it. Not the kind of flirtation intended to land me into his pants. But a little sweet talk can get a guy what he wants, and this guy wants me. For his article, anyway.

"Sure you do. You're a smart kid. What's your name?" I open, then close, my mouth. I'm not giving this guy my real name. "Okay, what do they call you out here? On the Block?"

Now I see my chance. *King of the Block*, the headline will read. *Snake Eyes, they call this mysterious young man in leather. Snake Eyes, because he sees all. This sexual outlaw rules what they call the Block, a tiny district where men swap currency for pleasure.* Maybe even a photo, full color, of me looking tough in my new used jacket. I could even find a biker's cap to match somewhere. I like that idea. "Everyone around here calls me..."

"BUTTERCUP!" A strident shout from across Franklin echoes between the facing townhouses. "YO. BUTTERCUP!"

Out of habit of responding to the nickname I hate, I make the mistake of turning my head. My buddy J.J. stands on the opposite curb, hands around his mouth. It's obvious he's summoning me. A trio of younger Black guys sitting on the steps behind him burst into laughter. I'm frozen in place. Everyone along the entire Block stares my way. It's that recurring nightmare of being naked at the chalkboard in math class all over again.

Even Winston Comstock the Third is struggling to keep a straight face. "They call you Buttercup?"

"No, it's…"

"BUTTERCUP!" God damn that J.J. When I turn around, hands stretched out in exasperation, he does a little dance. "Come over here, boy. We got to talk."

"I'm in the middle of something!" I yell.

"Hey, Buttercup. J.J.'s calling you." Bart, one of the other rent boys I've known a few weeks, gives Winston a good hard look as he sidles our way. He wets his lips and adjusts his trucker cap. He's wearing his usual costume of construction boots, a tank top, and an old red flannel shirt with the sleeves removed. With a world of meaning, he adds, "I can take over here, if you need."

"I don't need anything. Shoo. Shoo!" I wait until Bart vamooses. With apologies, I turn to the reporter. He's fished out a little pad and pen for notes. "Yeah, they call me…don't…it's only because my hair's so blond. Yellow, even. It's dumb."

"Nah, I get it. Buttercup suits you."

Well, fuck. Already, this is spinning out of control. Before J.J. can let out another of his deep-bellied roars, I stand and brush from my jacket the last remaining shreds of my dignity. "I don't think I can help you out," I tell the reporter. The obvious disappointment in his eyes doesn't help my resolve.

"You've got my card if you change your mind. I'm at the Hotel Jefferson for a couple more days. Number's on the back." But I'm already crossing to the other side of the Block, where my friend waits.

I met J.J. the week I got off the Greyhound from Galax. Bicentennial week. The whole damn town was covered in red, white, and blue. I already knew how to get a little dough for pleasing men, but I was a dopey kid who just didn't know where to find paying johns until one of my public park hookups pointed me in the direction of the Block, downtown.

And, of course, not knowing any better, I spent the first night walking on the wrong side of the street, wondering why none of the cars would stop. That's when a handsome Black guy took me by the shoulders and walked me to the other side of Franklin.

I can't even list all the stuff J.J. did when I arrived in town. He introduced me to the diner on the college campus nearby that's open late nights, where hustlers meet after hours to unwind over a cheap burger. The first time I got the clap, he pointed me to the free clinic. I'm pretty sure he even helped get my first place to stay, though I've moved plenty since. You won't find a more decent guy than J.J.

Except maybe when he's being an asshole, like now.

The entire time I'm dodging cars in the street, he's dancing on the curb and chanting my nickname. Tonight, he's wearing a snug pair of white shorts that make his skin seem somehow darker and that show off the enormous dick barely tucked inside. I've never seen the thing, but it's the biggest bulge on the Block. His shirt is a wild pattern of neon blues and yellows. Only the bottom two buttons are fastened, so anyone approaching him is sure to get an eyeful of a lotioned-up chest covered with coiled hairs. There's a pick in his back pocket for his tight and shiny Afro. J.J. is probably the oldest hustler out here, but nobody knows his real age. Thirty-five, maybe?

"Buttercup!" he says with a white-toothed grin as I finally approach. He holds out his right hand midair in an arm wrestling position, ready for a soul shake. The minute my hand is in his, though, he hauls me in, close. Pretending to give me a manly embrace, he growls in my ear, "What the fuck you talking to that interloper for?"

"He's a reporter." I'm confused. Was that why he'd mortified me in public?

"I know what he is." Through gritted teeth, he says, "And he's no good. Don't hang around men like that." The smile disappears. His eyes remain watchful, though. "It's okay. He's leaving." We both look after Winston Comstock as he shuffles down Franklin in the direction of the hotel. Once he's gone for good, J.J. drops the nice guy act and starts a lecture. "That man has been hitting up all the boys, trying to sniff out trouble for his magazine."

"Did he ask you?"

"Did he ask me? No, he did not ask me. He didn't ask any of us on this side of the street." When I turn my head each way, all the working boys within earshot are eavesdropping. J.J. clearly expects a response, but I don't have one. Am I supposed to apologize for a guy with a III behind his name being racist? Kinda seems to me like one goes with the other. "You gotta think it through. If he writes an article about us, it's just going to draw attention. The wrong kind of attention."

"He's going to write it anyway," I point out.

"So let him do it without you. He's trouble. Tell me you won't be helping him, Nicholas."

"All right!" I concede. "Fine. I won't help him. I've got rent to make tonight, anyway."

He lets out a genuine grin—not the false one he'd used when he'd called out my nickname for the whole damned world to hear. "That's what I like about my Buttercup. Pretty to look at and good sense to match."

"Aw." One of the things I hate about the fair skin that goes along with hair this blond is how it's obvious when I blush. I'm probably beet-red, just from a little bit of validation. "Anything for you."

"Anything, huh?" He gives me a long, slow wink and drapes one of his muscular arms around my shoulders. "Be careful. I might just take you up on that."

J.J. doesn't wear deodorant or cologne, but he has such a nice natural scent that I don't mind. Kind of like fresh laundry and...a flower I can't bring to mind. Sweet and summery. Something small and fragrant. A flash of yellow-gold. "You know where I live." I waggle my eyebrows.

He bites his lower lip in a sexy way. "Yeah, I do. You might come home some night and find this fine specimen in your bed, boy."

"Oh, I'd know how to handle a fine specimen if I did," I tell him, looking him sideways in the eye.

It's just good-natured banter. Neither of us means anything by it. Honestly, there's not a lot of recreational fucking going on between guys who walk the Block. At the end of the night, if I'm not starving, all I want is to head home and crash on my mattress. "Oh, you do, do you," J.J. is purring in my ear.

That's when the sedan pulls up. It's an older Duster, dark brown, with Three Dog Night playing on the AM radio. Since we're on the Black side of the Block, the driver has to lean over the passenger seat to roll down the window. "You fellas look like you're having a good time," he leers.

He's not attractive. It happens. In this business, not every customer looks like Paul Newman. Right now, we're getting more Gene Shalit—big plastic square-rimmed glasses, comical handlebar mustache, frizzy hair that's bigger than J.J.'s 'fro. Still, arm and arm, J.J. and I lean down to talk to the guy. "Maybe we are," I say. "You looking for a party?"

"I might be."

He doesn't have anything to add to that, so I glance up the street at the approaching traffic. It's the time of night when it's dark enough to bring out the first rush of horny men looking for fun, so to hurry things along, I try to make it appear as if I have other options—like in the car that's pulled up behind the Duster, a discreet distance away. "Well, let us know," I tell the stranger. "Maybe we can arrange a two-for-one discount."

Gene Shalit guy licks his lips. "I might have a taste for...Oreo action."

J.J. removes his arm from my shoulders. "Sir, an Oreo is two chocolate wafers and one creamy white filling, not the other way around."

The man's relentless in his metaphor, though. "Looks like you got more than enough chocolate for us both."

I keep a smile on my face, but—ick. J.J. isn't having any of it, though. "Aw, hell no," I hear him mutter beneath his breath. Then he's gone, walking down Franklin as quickly as he can.

"What's the matter with your friend?" the guy asks, clearly annoyed.

"He's in a mood."

"And you?"

I smile and lean further into the sedan. "In the mood."

"So, can we seal this deal?"

I glance around to see if anyone's looking. He does the same, checking the rear-view mirrors. "Show me your dick," I tell him. Cops won't whip out their dicks, see. That's entrapment. "C'mon. Show me what you're working with."

"I don't know..." He seems nervous, but his fingers toy with the fly of his brown slacks.

"I just want to see what I'm going to be sucking." Our eyes lock. "Let me see what I'll be taking deep down my throat. Or in other holes. You want that, right?" He nods, hypnotized by my patter. "Show me. I bet it's big." I watch as he unzips, then digs in his underwear. The entire time, he whips his head in every direction, nervous. At last, something emerges. It's little more than a pink worm flopping between his fingers. "Nice. Get it hard."

These suburban types like to be bossed around, I've found. They hate admitting their deviant urges come from within. But if they hear someone like me telling them to do things they've wanted to do all along—well, in their heads, nothing that follows is their fault.

"That's right. Show off that fat fucker." I'm being overgenerous in my praise, but my words make him swell in his clenched fist. "Think of all the dirty shit I'm going to do for you."

"Like what?"

"No kissing. I don't do that. Anything else goes."

"For the right price," he suggests, beating his dick with his fist. His other hand juts out the driver's window, making a motion.

I nod. "For the right price."

Then, suddenly, everything's confusion. Gene Shalit guy is stuffing his dick back into his pants and flashing a badge. A couple of plain-clothed bully boys leap from the car behind to manhandle and cuff and shove me up against the Duster so hard that my head bangs the frame. Somehow, the half-dollar in my jeans manages to get wedged sideways. It stabs into me like a knife. Lucky coin, my ass.

"He showed me his dick!" I'm yelling at the top of my lungs. "That buddy of yours *showed me his dick*!"

All the Black men on this side of the block have long since scattered. Over on the other side, the white guys are pretending not to see one of their own being busted. There's not even a sign of J.J., but I get it. I made the bad judgment call. I'm on my own. Someone's reading me my rights, then shoving me into the car, and pretty soon, I'm sitting in a splintery chair down at the local precinct.

"Your officer showed me his dick." Every time they try to get information out of me, I say it louder. The more times I make my point, the less likely they are to press charges. "It's illegal, and you know it. They'll throw any case right out!" When Mr. Shalit stumbles through the room, looking sheepish and angry, I shout it all again, adding, "*And it's a tiny little shrimp dick, too.*"

Finally, the booking officer has had enough. He heads off for a consultation with some of his colleagues. I've gotten under everyone's skin. "You got someone you can call to pick you up?" he sighs when he returns, obviously hoping to pass me off as quickly as possible.

I'm still cuffed, so I glare at him. "In there," I say, nodding down to my jacket pocket. Wary, the cop sticks two fingertips inside. He discovers the fold of bills first. He pushes them back down inside as we exchange a wry look. Then, he pulls out the business card.

"On the back," I tell him.

He nods, dials for me, then holds up the receiver.

The phone rings. Once. Twice. A click. I hear the theme song to *The Dukes of Hazzard* playing in the background. Then there's that deep voice, like butterscotch. "Hello?"

"Hey. It's Buttercup," I say, trying to ignore the amused smirk of the booking officer as he hangs onto the receiver for me. Yeah, fuck you and all your kind, motherfucker. "Listen. You help me, and I'll help you. Deal?"

MAKING RENT

Same day, close to midnight, and I'm sprawled face down across the back seat of a '76 Vega. My mouth's full of dick—this time, five and a half inches with a weirdly-flared head. Doesn't matter. I don't have to see the thing when it's battering my gullet. The guy's balls are so slack that they pool on the leatherette seat like they're melting.

"Fuckin' hot cock," I grunt, when I come up for breath. In the heat of the moment, I almost mean it. It's an okay cock. My working conditions would be better without the sickly maple syrup scent emanating from the guy's midsection. I know the smell. He's one of those fellows who never thinks to wash out his navel. I've turned down guys before for hygiene issues, but this one's minor enough to overlook.

"You like it?" he wants to know, peering down at me through his glasses. He's not anyone I've tricked with before. Late forties, stuffed into slacks and a too-tight short-sleeved dress shirt like he's got a midnight meeting with his manager. Belly like a Buddha, but I like that in a daddy.

"Love it, man. Big ol' dick. I want that load." I gulp wetly as I go down on him once more.

He pulls up the tails of his shirt to give me better access to the goods. "I don't look for cocksuckers too often." His voice is halfway between a whisper and a croak. "Mighta hit the jackpot here."

I come up once more from my attentions. "I'm the one who hit the jackpot, dude. Fat ol' slab of dick."

My words make him leap and twitch in my hand. "Is it really big?"

I look him in the eye, cocking my head as if surprised he could even ask such a thing. "You kidding me? You're huge."

"Yeah?"

He wants to believe. I give him permission. "Hell yeah!"

"Maybe you'd want it again?"

"Absolutely!" I agree. I love a repeat customer.

"I get so nervous about being caught, though."

"Just relax," I say, kneading his cock so that a glob of goo oozes from the tip. "My buddy's keeping an eye out. Right?"

From the front passenger seat comes Winston Comstock III's voice, hushed and deep. "All's clear." They're the first words he's said since we'd climbed into the man's car.

This gravel faculty parking lot on the downtown university's campus is always pretty much deserted at night. There's a streetlight nearby, but it hasn't worked well for the three years I've been bringing guys here in their cars. From time to time it flickers into wan life, then sputters out again. Now is one of those times; for a couple of seconds, I can see the reporter's patrician features in profile as he observes me at work. Interesting. I thought he might only listen. Since he's watching, though, I might as well put on a good show.

Though they're cracked open, the car windows begin to fog as the guy's breathing intensifies. My thumb and forefinger form a tight ring that slides to the base of the stranger's pole. My lips follow, forming an equally firm seal around my teeth. Forehead dislodging the guy's belly, I take him all the way down. Then my lips and fingers work in unison, up and down, in and out, giving the guy's rod as much sensation as he can take. From the corner of my eye, I can sense Winston's unwavering gaze. He wanted a story. I'll give him a story.

"Fuck." The john exhales the word like a prayer as he shoots into my welcoming mouth. The whole car bounces and shakes from his climax. Though he tries to buck away when he comes—he probably has a wifey at home who won't let him sully her tonsils with his seed—I don't let him. I make him deliver every drop of that nectar onto my tongue and don't relent until he's done.

While he recuperates from the shock, I watch the silent parade of emotions across his features: relief, happiness, then a bit of self-consciousness. "We've gotta do that again," he says, chuckling. "Bring your friend along. It's hot to be watched."

"Look for me anytime, handsome," I tell him, only ducking away when I see his lips pucker up and seek mine.

"You told him his penis was large." I'd warned Winston not to take notes while I worked. Now we're back on the steps of the Y; he's scribbling like a madman. I nod, though I'm privately snickering at his over-delicacy. "Was it? Compared to other...patrons?"

"Patrons? Christ. We call them johns. Or clients. No, it wasn't, really. Is yours?"

He ignores me. "So, you lied to him?"

"No!"

"You didn't tell him the truth."

His line of questioning makes me a little cranky. He doesn't get it. "If you order dinner at the Howard Johnson's and the chick cashing you out says, *Hope you have a nice day, hon*, do you interrogate her ass to see if she's being sincere? Or if your tailor at Brooks Brothers says those expensive shirts suit you, do you call the guy a liar? Paying a courtesy or two is part of the job."

Scribble, scribble. "You seem defensive."

Shaking my head, I start looking for the next trick. There's still rent to make. "It's customer service, okay? Just because my customers are looking to shoot a load doesn't make my little white lies...I don't know. Immoral. Not more than any other service job." No reply, but he seems to consider what I'm saying for a moment before jotting more notes. I picture the article. *Until that night, this reporter never considered that the sexual outlaw abides by a code of decency of his own, a moral compass honed by the street.* "So. Is *yours* large?"

"Is my what...?" When I waggle my eyebrows and nod at the lump in his slacks, he shakes his head. "I'm straight, man."

As if so-called straight guys can't have big dicks, too.

⟡

IT'S ACTUALLY DEAD EASY TO CONVINCE JOHNS TO let Winston tag along. "This gentleman likes to watch," I tell them. Then I offer to knock a twenty off my regular price if they allow him. Of course, I jack up my regular price by fifteen so that I'm only losing five bucks out of the deal, but not a single prospect has said no, especially when they see Winston dressed like a respectable Ivy League poly sci professor.

Now I'm in a third-story walk-up flat with one of the locals. A lot of gays have made the area around the Block into their own little village, but most of them don't shop where they live, if you get what I'm saying. This older fellow, though, had been sitting on his front steps over on Main when Winston and I had passed. He's not a bad-looking guy. Just tired, like he'd just gotten home from his waiter or bartending job at a yuppie hotspot. Lean, balding a little. Takes care of himself, though. "Would you model for me?" he'd asked after I gave him a nod and a friendly smile. Then, "How much?"

Modeling is simple. I stand in the middle of a worn Oriental carpet, wearing nothing more than my jockstrap and white socks, pressing the flats of my hands together to make my pecs pop. Slowly, I revolve around and around, maintaining eye contact with the guy when I can. When I can't, I stare dead at Winston where he sits on the bench of an antique parlor organ across the room, daring him to look away.

He doesn't.

This apartment is chock a block with old lady furniture. Dusty old antiques, ancient sewing machines, ornate mirrors everywhere, spindly tables piled high with leather-bound books. My john sits in a velvet armchair adorned with a doily. He sits naked upon a tea towel spread over the seat, pinching his nipples while his hand furiously beats his meat. From time to time, he'll issue an order in a flat voice. "Bend over," he'll say, or maybe, "Spread those ass cheeks."

I smile like the Mona Lisa and do as he says. It's an easy job, becoming a blank screen on which men project their fantasies. From his eyes, I deduce which parts of me turn him on the most. The thick curve of my butt. My big calves. My pecs, when I rub my hands across them. When I stretch, the fur of my pits that teases the edges of my triceps.

I'm not my own type. Believe me, when you grow up around an extended family of Swedes and all the men look like big ol' butch blond bruisers, you get sick of the sight. His excitement makes me feel hot, though. Beautiful, even.

The thick inches in his fist swell redder the longer he watches. His sticky noises grow louder. I can smell that precum from several feet away. With a long, slow tease, I pull down my jock and let my junk loose. My own dick is three-quarters hard. Enough to show off the length, not enough to make it stand up straight. It and my big old balls dangle over the waistband so that when I tug at the elastic from both sides, everything flops and dances. The john groans and gives one of his tits a savage tug.

"You want it?" I ask him in a low voice as I brandish my hardening meat.

He nods, opening wide. I close the space between us to sink my dick deep into his warm, welcoming mouth. Immediately his head begins to bob, so desperate is he to gobble me to the root. At this distance, I can take over nipple duty. Between my fingers, his toughened nubs feel like pencil erasers. The more cruelly I twist and pinch them, the harder and better he sucks. His own hand beats faster. The stranger's hot breath sears my cock.

And what's Winston making of this exhibition? On the organ bench, his posture remains impeccable, his face impassive to the point of stone. Now, with my client's eyes closed as blindly he jogs the last lap toward his own pleasure, the reporter is my sole audience. I'm not content to give him a view of only the jiggling mounds of my butt, though. I angle my hips so that he witnesses the whole show: my seven inches pistoning the guy's lips, my balls slapping against his chin, the force of my hands cradling his skull. I want Winston Comstock III to spectate every sloppy thrust. He wanted a story about the hustlers of the Block. This is what we do.

For a long moment, our eyes meet. I celebrate our conspiracy with a wink.

He turns his head as if he's had enough. Yet when my john erupts with a roar a moment later, Winston can't help but stare. And I can't help but notice how his hand moves to his crotch, pauses, then curls into a fist. It's as if he wanted to shove down on the erection hiding behind that plaid bulge, to bring pleasure to his painful constriction—but thought the better of it when he realized I was watching.

Yeah, I see you, Ivy League.

❧

"YOU'RE NOT TIRED?" HE ASKS, TWO QUICK backseat blowjobs and a handy later. The last john has dumped us out in front of the library. Dried autumn maple leaves rustle above. They're as restless as I am, this hour of the morning.

"Call it a night if you want," I tell him. "I'm dog tired, but..."

"You're staying out for more?"

I shrug. "Last call is at two. Johns find their way here after the bars close. I can get another hundred bucks if I hustle my ass."

"Gotta make that rent money."

"Gotta make that rent money," I repeat. His notebook is out and poised, but it's too dark for him to write.

"Maybe you could have saved up earlier in the month?"

"Thanks, Dad." Seriously? Will I get advice on blue-chip stocks next?

"Is that what your dad would say?"

Even in the gloom, I sense his eyes glinting as if he's onto a hot story. *Who is this devilish rogue, this Snake Eyes, who prowls the street at an hour when most of us sleep? From what past is he trying so desperately to escape?* "I had the money," I tell him in a level voice. "Then I didn't." No response to that one. Guilt pricks at me. I hope I haven't been too spiky. "How long are you in town?"

"Not much longer."

Now I'm anxious. He can't leave. Not yet. I want to give him a better show than the penny-ante tricks I've turned tonight. I try to stay casual as I say, "I've got a big job lined up tomorrow night. He'll let you watch. For your story. If you wanted, you know."

"Big job?" I've piqued his curiosity. "How so?"

"Come see. It'll be worth it."

His jaw works silently from side to side. Our eyes meet and hold for longer than they should. "All right," he says with the slightest of grins. "I'm in."

I watch as he strides off in the direction of the Jefferson. It's only a minute or two later, when I cross over to the Block, that I see J.J. on the opposite curb, leaning against the streetlight. He's not striking one of his pickup poses...not the tough street guy, or the friendly jock who happens to be out late. No, it looks like he's been watching me and doesn't like what he saw. "Yo!" I call with the excitement of running across a friend as I raise my hand.

But now that he's spotted me with Winston. J.J. just shakes his head and disappears into the shadows.

STRAIGHT AS AN ARROW

How do I describe my regular client, Benjamin? He resembles that cartoon owl on TV who wants to know how many licks it takes to get to the center of a Tootsie Pop, only human and with a big ol' dick. Like an owl, he's stout and sports big eyes set in a face that's always alert. Then there's the unkempt beard that's grizzled, gray, and sticks out at all kinds of crazy angles—just like the whiskers protruding from his ears. Dressed, he looks very much like the former family doctor he was before retirement. Undressed...well, not a lot of people think of doctors as having a rocking body. Benjamin might still look like that wise old lollipop-crunching owl from the neck up, but the chin down part could model for *Drummer* magazine.

And did I mention that monster dick? The thing's thick as a forearm and redder than a poker left in the fire. He's told me before he likes to work it with a vacuum pump, but honest to God, I don't see how he even stuffs it in the tube. Now he's nudging that tennis ball knob against my quivering hole, and like every time I meet the guy, I don't think I can take it.

In fact, I say aloud, "I don't think I can take it."

Through my slitted eyes, I see Winston in the corner of the room, trying to appear both comfortable and casual on a metal folding chair as he rests his elbows on his knees. One hand covers his mouth; the other nurses a can of beer. What's he thinking over there? *Could it be that Snake Eyes, fearless champion of the sidewalks, has met his match? Will he rise to the challenge offered by this seasoned predator?*

Above me, Benjamin grins before shoving me further onto his homemade fuck bench. It's built like a picnic table, only all the surfaces are covered with a soft shag carpet. I'm kneeling on the lower board, ass at his dick level, high in the air. My chest rests on the tabletop. Three bottoms could kneel side by side on this bench. They probably have. "Oh, you'll take it, son," he growls. I whimper when he slaps three fingers' worth of Crisco on my hole, adding to the gooey mix already there. "You'll take it, and you'll love it."

"Yes, sir." Benjamin pays me better than average. For one thing, I need to take a bus or cab all the way out here to the city's west end, where the houses are large and brick and colonial, the trees grow dense and wild, and the sidewalks are few. I've saved a few bucks tonight by having Winston drive us in his rental car. It's not just the transportation that Benjamin pays extra for, though. The old man likes to be in complete control of a pretty boy a few decades his junior. I'm expected to comply with his every whim. Luckily, our sexual drives synch up pretty well.

There's a short length of chain connecting the

leather cuffs shackling my wrists. Benjamin has threaded one link through a sturdy eye hook on the bench's underside to keep me in place. Occasionally, I make a show of pretending to struggle. The chain makes a satisfying ruckus whenever I rattle it. Now, I create an absolute racket, feigning panic at his blunt weapon forcing open my guts. Maybe my reaction isn't entirely make-believe: the good doctor's dick feels like a baseball bat going in. Even though I've got the Crisco keeping me slippery, my eyes still water as he shoves in inch after inch of that meaty hog. My grunting as I try to accommodate him isn't pretend, either.

"That's right," he says. I can hear the grin in his voice. He's relishing my distress. "Be a good boy, now. You want to be my good boy, don't you?"

"Yes, sir. I do." He's only a couple of inches in, and already every nerve in my body jangles like chimes in a wind shear. "It's just that you're so goddamned big."

"But you love it."

"I fucking love it," I breathe with my face buried in the fuck bench's carpet.

Now I'm panting. He's not making it easy for me. I hear the retort of his cupped palm on my ass before I feel the actual slap. Prickly heat blooms where he connects. The shock makes me gasp and open wider, as he intends. Another couple of inches slide inside. By now, I don't have to play-act anything. My wrists struggle helplessly against their bonds; I let out a low, feral groan that fills the cellar room. "That's it," he says, rapt by the vision of his saber piercing my twitching, puckering hole. I wish to hell I could see what he was seeing. "Almost there."

I swear I can feel the prominent ridge of his cock head scraping my guts. I'm approaching that point of transition, though, when the struggle promises to yield to pure pleasure. My anticipation opens me even wider. "Please." My whimpering is genuine by this point. "Please let me have it."

I hear Benjamin chuckle. "You'll get it," he promises. Then, "You." He's talking to Winston, who's remained at the sex room's distant perimeter. "Come look at this."

I'm so far over the bench at this point that I can't see what's going on, but I hear the reporter clear his throat and say, softly and politely, "That's not really necessary."

"No, come on. You like to watch, right? You've gotta see this." Benjamin has clearly swallowed my story that the man I've brought into his house is a voyeur. "I said, come look."

I hear the metal chair scrape and then the sounds of loafers shuffling over concrete. Even a *Newsweek* reporter with a WATS line obeys Benjamin when he issues a command. "I'd prefer..."

While they debate, I'm left teetering over the axis between agony and joy, helpless to shift from one to the other. "Look at this big ol' dick splitting that boy pussy open. Beautiful sight, isn't it?" Benjamin clearly expects agreement. "Watch." He shoves in a fraction of an inch more, causing my legs to buckle and my back to arch. "The kid loves it. He fucking needs it. You sure you don't want a go?"

With the driest of tones, I hear Winston demur. "I'm good, thanks."

Of course, I'm disappointed. But I don't get much time for regret, because Benjamin makes a final push to batter my last resistances. His thick pubes grind against my ass. That does it. My head jerks back, and I let out a roar. The man's fleshy knob hammers my prostate, and damn, does it feel good. Every slow thrust stokes my inner furnace to a white heat. "Look at this boy," snarls Benjamin, giving my butt another sharp slap. "He's a regular dick pig. But whose dick do you love the best?"

"Yours, sir!" Through genuine tears, I struggle to see what Winston might be doing. It's tough to focus when each collision of the older man's hips against mine jangles my chains and abrades my chest against the carpet surface. I've got the reporter's attention, though. He's staring down at the spot where Benjamin and I connect, absolutely fixated upon the man's monster dick stretching me out. It feels thick as a tree trunk, that cock.

I feel Benjamin's hand on my shoulder to yank me back. I'm alternating so quickly between pleasure and pain that the two extremes blur. All I know is that I want as much of both as he can dish out. Benjamin's never a long-laster. I can already tell he's building up to a ball-busting climax by the wheeze of his chest. Maybe Winston's proximity turns him on. I don't know. Tonight, he's especially riled up. I don't mind since I know there'll be an encore after his climax. "Fuck me," I moan, spreading my legs as far as they'll open. "Use that hole."

"Oh, I am," he mutters, giving the already-red mounds a slap. Good thing I'm enjoying the hell out of what he's doing. I couldn't escape the fuck bench if I wanted to. "Using that hole real hard."

"Make it yours."

Good thing, too, that we're in his basement because his bellowing would otherwise wake the neighborhood. The force of his climax propels the bench forward several inches. For a panicked moment, I envision it toppling over and me unable to do anything to prevent the crash. But then, while his semen burns at the entrance of my sore hole, he lets out a giant nasal snort and pulls out with an audible squelch.

"Damn, you're a good boy." He gives my quivering ass a last slap as he stumbles around the bench to unhook me. "Look at that hole gape." He's addressing Winston. "Ever seen anything prettier?" I don't hear a reply, but it doesn't matter. I gaze at Benjamin with gratitude when he rids me of the cuffs around my wrists. I'm loose but not yet free. "You know what comes next."

"Yes, sir." Though my legs are unsteady, I toddle over to the corner of the cellar where Benjamin has installed an open shower. There I lower myself to the tiles, over the floor drain. Knees spread, hands covering my hard dick and balls, I grovel before the man towering above.

"You ready?" he asks. I nod as he positions himself. The man turns to beckon Winston over. "You're gonna want to see this part," he says with a snicker. "Come on, now. Don't be shy."

I catch the reporter's eye as he dutifully shuffles over. He has no idea what's about to happen.

"Open wide." My lips part, and my eyes squeeze shut. I've learned the hard way that lids closed is the better choice. "Ladies and gents...here we go."

After the softest of sighs, the old man lets loose. There's a second of anticipation before I feel his warm jet of liquid splattering my face. Benjamin's tank is full after those Buds and all that stimulation; I gasp in real pleasure as he sprays a seeming bucket of his piss onto my face.

Pale urine sprays everywhere. Up my nostrils, where its metallic scent seems to linger. Into my open, waiting mouth, tasting only like stale water with only the faintest tang of the brew he's been chugging. Down my chest. Onto my stomach and down to where my hands cup my junk. It splashes onto the tiles with a thousand tiny patters and sloshes from my body. Just when I think he's done, there's another hard squirt. Then another. A third, weaker. Then it's over. At last, I can open my eyes and stare up at the man who gifted me the contents of his bladder.

"Good boy," he says, patting the top of my head. It's about the only place that didn't get wet.

"Thank you, sir." This is how all my evenings with Benjamin end. A fuck, a hosing down, then a quick shower and an envelope of twenties on the way out. I'm about to stumble to my feet and grope for the faucet handle behind when he surprises me, though.

"Your turn, buddy," he informs Winston.

It takes a moment for the words to sink in. For both of us. I fall once more to my knees, stunned. Winston shakes his head. "What?"

"Your turn." Benjamin nods at me. "Piss on him."

"I'm not going to...you can't expect me..." It's the first time I've seen Winston drop the impartial reporter act. Until now, nothing has taken him aback.

"Fuck yeah, I do!" roars our host. "Whaddaya think I gave you that beer for?"

I raise up on my haunches a little. *It's okay*, I

mouth, nodding to encourage him. Surely, he won't do anything stupid to jeopardize my payday. The reporter and I exchange a mute exchange of expressions, his intended to convey discomfort and refusal. Mine are a little more animated as I try to mime that he should shut the fuck up and get it over with.

Back and forth we struggle without words until at last I speak. "Just do it."

"You're not getting out of here without pissing on my boy." Benjamin sounds genial, but he means what he says.

Winston wears the expression of a trapped man. Maybe he is. I hadn't known Benjamin would expect anything of him—but neither am I protesting. For a second, bitterness warps those refined features. It evaporates quickly, though. His lids half-close and his face becomes impassive. "Yeah. Okay. Whatever." His fingers fumble with the fabric of his slacks. He's angry. Trust me, I've lived with a father and enough older brothers and uncles to know when a straight man is tamping down his rage. "I'll piss on him. I'll piss all over the little shit."

I don't even get a chance to see that boarding school dick. He's scarcely yanked open the gap in his tighty whities to pull it out when a stream of urine hits me squarely in the eye. I gasp and blink them closed, but it's too late. It hurts. And if I thought Benjamin's bladder was full, it's nothing compared to what's cascading out of Winston. Fuck. I've never had an actual horse piss on me, but this is pretty much what I imagine it's like: a firehose battering me with acrid liquid until, after what feels like minutes have passed, the pipes give out.

I'm still blinking and sputtering and trying to

clear my eyes when Benjamin tosses me a hand towel. My vision clears just in time to see a pair of legs in plaid trousers and loafers stomping up the cellar stairs, making a hasty getaway. The door slams. Then he's gone.

Benjamin plops his hairy ass down on the fuck bench and lights up a Marlboro. "Kind of a weirdo," he decrees, taking a deep drag to fill his lungs with smoke. Then he breathes out twin columns from his nostrils. "But he puts on a damn good show."

AT MY KNOCK, HE OPENS HIS HOTEL DOOR ALMOST immediately. "What the fuck, dude?" I shove my way inside. "Ben had to bring me back. Now I owe him one."

Winston, still dressed in his Brooks Brothers camouflage, makes a show of trying to keep me out. I'm in a mood, though, and have the advantage of surprise. "How'd you get my room number?"

"Oh, come on." That's beside the point. "The Jefferson night clerk lets us trick in the lobby men's room if you tip him right. Why'd you abandon me?"

He shuts his door then stalks past me to retrieve his billfold from the nightstand, so I won't make off with it, which I pretend not to both notice and resent. I've been in the Hotel Jefferson rooms many a time with clients. Forty years ago, they might have been the peak of luxury for this town, but now they're stodgy and dated. Clean, though. "Go home."

I see that he's got his suitcase on the bed, already half-packed. Uh-oh. "Not 'til I get answers."

"Get out." He points to the door, but the threat

doesn't carry much force. "I swear to God, I'll call someone. The desk clerk. The police."

"Sure, go ahead." I remove my leather jacket, fold it in half, and lay it upon the white bedclothes, cool as anything. "Make a ruckus. Let everyone find you with a known rent boy in your hotel room. See how that goes for you." I can see in his eyes and by the slump of his shoulders that, for now, I've won the battle. I nod at the half-packed suitcase. "You were just going to leave town?" He nods, crossing his arms and silently daring me to object. "Why? Because of a little piss?"

"Why? Seriously?" Now he's pacing back and forth, an animal in its cage. "Why? Because you made me part of my story, kid. That's why." I shake my head, not understanding. His words fly through the air like aimed darts. "I'm supposed to be objective. That's a reporter's whole...I can't be objective if you're...*involving me* in your...shenanigans."

"You wanted to see what my life was like."

"See, yes. It stops there. I've got an ethical duty. I can't be part of my stories."

"It's unethical to whip out your willy and piss on a hustler?" I commence the sentence with a note of incredulity, but by the time I reach its end...yeah, it kind of makes sense. I shift strategies. "You didn't have to do it. You're a big boy. You could've said no. Walked out, if you really felt uncomfortable. But you didn't. Nobody held a gun to your head. You got it out and pissed on me. It's just piss. I didn't take it personally. Not until you left."

This is the right tack. He flops down in an armchair, defeated, and shakes his head. "What do you want from me?"

"Take me with you." I'm as surprised at the words as he is. I'd never expected to say any such thing. "Take me up north, to the city. Find me a place to live. See me when you can. Make me part of your story."

His eyes glitter, hard and cold. He shakes his head. "You have entirely misinterpreted..."

Yet I'm certain I haven't. "You wanna talk ethics? Because it seems pretty unethical to me to follow a streetwalker to all his tricks and watch what happens, up close. Real close. What'd you do, come back here and think about me after? Did it excite you? Did you touch yourself under those fancy sheets, Winston?" He turns his head, sets his jaw. I'm dancing on a knife's edge here. From the bed, I drop onto my knees, where I shuffle across the hotel carpet until I'm at his feet, within an arm's reach. "All those things you watched, I can do for you. Let me." He shifts uncomfortably in his seat, still refusing to look my way. "Put me in some little shithole flat and visit me when you want. Any time. I'll be what you want me to be. Tough guy, sweet guy...anything you can dream."

"I'm straight."

Yeah, I've heard him say that before. Know what I'm not hearing, though? The word *no*. "I'll never forget that. I get it!" I move a little closer and embolden myself to reach out. Though his gaze remains steadily fixed on the hallway door, he doesn't object when I tug at the leather of his belt. It glides through the buckle like a knife through butter. "I respect straight guys. But you've seen me, Winston. You know I can keep a secret."

Is it my imagination, or does he actually lift his

hips a little so I can loosen the prong from its hole? His Adam's apple bobs as he swallows, hard.

I'm treating him as gently as any mother with her baby, keeping my voice soft and reassuring as I proceed. "I wouldn't bother you, wouldn't make any claims. I don't nag. I'd be someone you can rely on. For the good stuff. Only for the good stuff." He's unzipped now. Part of me can't believe he's let me get this far. The other part, more cynical, gloats and thinks, *Told you so*. "Lift?"

At my suggestion, his hips inch into the air. I tug his pants down his thighs, overbuilt calves covered with a surprising growth of fur the same reddish shade as his hair. Now that those baggy trousers aren't in the way, I can see he's rock-hard in his BVDs. My fingers dare to press against the length of him, kneading softly, like a nursing kitten.

"I'd never steer you wrong, buddy." The tips of my fingers grapple with the elastic, towing down as once more he raises his hips to accommodate me. At no point does he actually look my way. Does he feel hypnotized? Is he trying to disassociate himself from what's happening? A lot of my work is giving men permission to do the things they want, never requiring they put their desires into words. I know Winston needs me to initiate. What he doesn't want is to ruin his straight-as-an-arrow persona by asking for something taboo.

The sight of his dick fills me with lust. If I get my way, I am going to know that cock very, very well over the next few months. Though average in length, it's concrete hard to the point that it's difficult for me to pry the warm flesh away from his abdomen. I wrap my fingers around him and squeeze so I can admire the flare of the purple-red head. At my touch, his neck lolls back, and his legs spread. Silently I admire his square chin from underneath and let go of his dick only long enough to undo his lowermost shirt buttons.

"I love this cock," I whisper, then take the time to study it. Big, hairy bull balls. Pubes more brown than red. I'd never suspected the man would be covered in fur. "I'm going to make this cock feel very, very good."

Winston's eyes remain steadfastly shut as I hunker down to take him. Slowly, very slowly, I widen my mouth around the six-inch shaft to let him feel the heat of my breath on his skin. His dick jumps and twitches against the roof of my mouth.

"This will be *my* cock," I announce, suddenly possessive. Then I close my lips and engulf it with my wet tongue and cheeks, taking it to the base.

He barks out his pleasure, so astonished at the glorious sensations I provide that I wonder if the wifey ever sucks him at all. My fingers curl around his heavy nuts, tugging them, multiplying his pleasure, as my mouth begins a slow, deliberate journey up and down Winston's shaft. Already, he's squirting salty precum onto my tonsils. Small wonder, with all the sex shows I've been giving him these last couple of nights.

I am determined to make him want more of me. One by one, I pull out all the stops—the deep throating of his dick to the root, the careful attention I pay his nuts with my tongue, the steady pressure I apply in a circle around the base to keep him at his hardest. None of that verbal B.S. about how big he is. I don't want him to think I'm doing him a courtesy, like for a client. I want the man to know that this moment is all about him. His needs. What he wants.

I want him to know that this is how it could be from now on.

And Winston is loving it. *Loving* it. The longer I go, the more helpless he becomes. His hands flutter and jerk a few inches above the armrests, uncertain what to do. They alight on his chest, then at his sides, as if he hopes to stuff them into the pockets he's forgotten are now around his ankles. Eventually, I feel his fingers in my hair, then his caress at the back of my head. Then, at long last, he looks down at me and what I'm doing to him.

He's in the moment now, a full participant in our forbidden act. My eyes have to do the smiling for me when I gaze up at him, my mouth stuffed with his married dick. He holds my chin. Strokes the sides of my cheeks. As I step up the pace, he begins to direct my mouth, showing me where to suck, when to hold still, when to increase my pace.

For long minutes, I minister to the man, giving him the attention he so obviously craves. I swear I'm not trying to finish him off when the fingers of my left hand begin to probe in the vicinity of his hole, but the attention there causes him to groan like a man out of control. One of his hands clutches hard around my wrist and forces me in, telling me without words what he wants. The second I make contact with his red-hot pucker, he begins shooting.

Winston shoves my skull down on his cock while he convulses and writhes. The man shoots as heavily as he pisses. I've got thick seed painting the back of my throat, so thick and copious that it oozes from the sides of my mouth as I continue to gulp on his meat. I choke and swallow what I can, but it's not until he releases me and I settle back on my haunches, moisture fogging my eyes, that I'm able to devour what remains. I wipe off my face on my forearm.

I look up to discover Winston regarding me with clear eyes. I hazard the slightest of smiles. He nods. The gesture's almost imperceptible, but it fills my heart with hope. I have a chance, after all.

"You liked that." My statement is rewarded with another tiny nod. Moved by what emotion, I don't know, I rise so that we're face to face. More than anything, I want his lips on mine, his tongue in my mouth. It's the one act I won't perform for clients, no matter how much cash they offer. That kind of intimacy, I tell myself, has to mean something. I have to have one thing that means something.

Yet at the last possible second, he jerks away his head. Once again, he becomes distant. "No kissing." That butterscotch voice is flat and emotionless. "I'm straight."

I'm taken aback. But I hide my disappointment. "Let me come by tomorrow morning," I urge as he heaves himself to his feet and pulls up his trousers. Sounding playful and keeping it light, I add, "It can be a real interview. Or other stuff, if you prefer." Front button fastened, he disappears into the bathroom. I have to stop him from closing the door completely to say, more seriously, "You see how I could be part of your story from now on. Right?"

Our eyes meet. After a moment, his slither away. He nods at the wall, not saying anything.

"I'll come in the morning," I promise to the bathroom door as it shuts. Then I gather my jacket and exit the hotel room.

Already, I'm making giddy plans. I won't show up with everything packed, ready to head back to the Big Apple with my new beau. I'm not that much of a bumpkin. The most I'm really hoping for is a promise and maybe enough bus fare to get me up north. Maybe by Halloween. Though it wouldn't hurt, maybe, to stuff my best clothing into a laundry bag and have it ready to go by my apartment door, just in case. Definitely, I should dress nicely. My one good white dress shirt, the black jeans, my shiny black shoes. Again, just in case. Winston won't want to travel with someone who looks like a thug.

When I step out into the night, I don't even think about going back on the Block. With the scent of Winston Comstock III lingering on my upper lip, I practically skip home. The soaring disco melodies from the apartments above play the ecstatic sound-track for my heart.

❧

"HE CHECKED OUT," SAYS THE CLERK AT THE Jefferson front desk the following morning. He mistakes my frozen gaze as a demand for more information. "Late last night. Not that it's any of your business," he declares, looking me up and down with meaning before turning his back on me.

Of course, Winston has hightailed home. Of fucking course he has. Because that's all my luck ever buys. Because, like my father would always tell me, life is always, always going to make me eat shit. Shit is all I'll ever deserve.

Fuck. Know what? I don't even deserve this fancy shirt. It's with anger that I start ripping off the ugly, constraining thing. During my struggle, a button actually pops off and flies behind the counter. The snooty clerk turns to watch it hit the floor. He raises an eyebrow. "Here. All yours," I snarl, throwing the tangle in his surprised face. Then, I stomp out of the ritzy lobby and into the unfamiliar light of day.

FAIRYLAND

I didn't cry. Not once in the weeks following did I shed a tear over Winston Comstock III, his tasseled loafers, his fancy clothing, or the things he'd let me do to him. I couldn't mourn for something that never was, same as I couldn't will a whole new way of life into being. Mostly what I felt was stupid. I was one hundred percent that big dumb ox everyone thought. So, I kept off the Block for a week, sitting in my basement room eating not much more than cereal from the box, wondering where I could go or who would take me.

Then J.J. appeared.

One night I startled to a pounding on my door, loud enough to rouse the dead. Even though I wasn't wearing anything more than pajama bottoms, I took down the security bar, undid the deadlock, pulled back the bolt, and opened the door as far as the chain would allow. J.J. shook his head and said, "I've been looking all over for your ass. Let me in."

I obeyed, but he didn't stay long. I guess the sight of all those empty Sugar Smacks boxes lying around rendered him speechless, because all he could do was stare at the squalor with a dropped jaw. Then he'd held up a finger. "Don't go anywhere. I will be right back. But get in the shower, boy. You're ripe."

I made a half-hearted effort to clean up in my sink with a washcloth. Not having a bath or shower is the reason this room's so cheap—I've gotten by taking them at the Y or at a john's place. Ten minutes later, J.J. returned bearing a greasy bag from the local burger joint. It was the first food I'd eaten in a long time that didn't come in a box featuring a cartoon character, and the smell was so good that it made my stomach roar. I abandoned all manners and ripped into them while he watched.

When I was done, he crossed his arms and regarded me from across my wobbly table. "You want to talk?" I shook my head, feeling guilty. The man had just bought me a whole sack of cheeseburgers, after all. "All right," he said. "That's okay. I'll just sit here with you for a little. When you're ready to talk, you'll talk."

Night after night, he returned, staying for a couple of hours, burning up some of his prime cruising hours for my sake. Usually, he brought food just to make sure I had something to eat. Once, he brought a little portable black-and-white TV that he left on my table so we could watch sitcoms together.

Once, he even gathered all my dirty sheets and clothing and returned from the automat later with everything folded and clean. I let him help me make up the mattress on the floor. Then we lay atop it, him the big spoon, me the little. It's nice to be held, in the quiet.

Sweet as it is to know someone gives a shit, I've still got rent to pay. And a Y membership to maintain. My body can't survive on sugar cereal and charity burgers forever, either—plus, there's the money I try to send home to my mama on the sly each month so she can treat herself to a little something.

So, after a few days, I hit the streets and get back to work.

⊗

IT'S THE DEAD OF WINTER WHEN J.J. SHOWS UP AT my place shortly after dusk. New year. New decade, even. I'm getting dressed for the night ahead—plaid flannel shirt, tight jeans, boots, with a red puffer vest to keep me warm—when I hear my friend's familiar knock on the door. Once inside, he takes off his jacket and looks around. "You got yourself a bed frame," he says with surprise. "Will wonders never cease!"

"Yeah, I thought I'd try this thing called, wait a minute, it'll come to me...saving up for shit?" At least I get a chuckle out of him. All my attention focuses, though, on the column of glossy stock rolled up in his left fist. A magazine, I realize. "Is that what I think?"

J.J. lets out a deep sigh. "You might want to sit down."

"Show me."

He tosses the *Newsweek* onto my little table, where it unfurls, cover up. Some pretty blonde stares up at me. *A Star for the 80s: Meryl Streep*, it says. I manage to slide into one of the chairs, but I can't summon the strength to move my arms. "Is it bad?"

J.J. sits down opposite. "It's way in the back."

When I do nothing, he flips to a spot that falls open easily, as if it's been creased to this page before. "It's not even a full article."

I can see what he means. The main story is something called *Homosexual Activists: The Gay Frontier,* with a byline I don't recognize. There are a couple of companion pieces offset to the sides. *On the Block,* one of them says. Winston's name is set in bold type underneath. "Is it bad, though?"

He closes his mouth. "I shouldn't have shown you."

"No." My voice sounds unnaturally high. "Read it to me."

"You sure?" I nod. "All right then." J.J. clears his throat, picks up the magazine, and begins. "*Men in the know call it the Block. A deceptive, innocuous sobriquet for one of the many sordid fleshpots spreading like cancer across American small cities. Here, hustlers prowl in packs, hoping to relieve customers of legal tender and dignity alike. And foremost among this...*" He swallows and looks my way. "You doing all right?"

"Go on," I demand. Like ripping a bandage from a hairy place, I tell myself. A few seconds of agony, then it'll be over.

"*...foremost among this fairyland for fairies is the mincing parody of masculinity who calls himself Buttercup. Pansy might be more appropriate. This small-change hustler, a sex deviant who extracts cash from his victims for what many would consider nauseating carnal...*"

"What the fuck!" I yell. The table skids as I jolt to my feet.

J.J. makes an appeal to my better nature after he makes sure the little TV is okay. "Calm down, now. You know it ain't right. You don't mince."

"No, you don't get it." I wave my hands furiously as I arrange my thoughts. "That line is mine. I said it to him when we met. I pointed out all the lights and music from the townhouses and said the Block's a regular fairyland for fairies. This dipshit can't even write his own gags."

There's a half-smile on J.J.'s handsome face. We've spent a lot of time together, the last few weeks. How come I haven't noticed how good looking he is? "Motherfucker," he breathes.

I'm grinning like crazy now, maybe for the first time in months. "Stupid-ass closeted motherfucker," I correct.

"Plagiarizing stupid-ass closeted motherfucker..."

"That William F. Buckley, Jr. wannabe, plagiarizing, stupid-ass, closeted, cheating, sad sack of shit motherfucker who cannot even write his own turns of phrase and has to steal them from the *pansies* he despises." My sigh is of vicious satisfaction. That Ivy League asshole had done his worst, but you know what? The bandage is ripped and gone. He can't hurt me any longer. "Can you believe that mess?"

"What're you going to do about him?"

"Nothing."

J.J. raises his eyebrows, surprised. "You could call *Newsweek*. Demand a retraction. Maybe even sue. Defamation of character!"

"Nah. Fuck him." I mime crumpling a ball of paper and tossing it into the wastebasket by the door. "Fuck him and his sorry-ass sham marriage. Fuck his Brooks Brothers shirts, his Vidal Sassoon haircut..."

"Boy did have a cute ass, though," J.J. says, now the mood's lighter.

I shrug. "His dick was pretty good, too."

"Oh?" This was a detail I had not shared. He shakes his head and laughs aloud as he stands, rolls up the magazine, and stuffs it in his back pocket. Then he reaches for the denim jacket he'd earlier spread across the chair. "All right then. You're not flying off the handle, at least."

"Don't go," I tell him. A table lies between us, but it doesn't have to. I move near and voice the question I should've asked weeks ago. "Why have you been taking such good care of me?"

"Why...?" His attention slips sideways. "Old curs like me gotta look after the young pups. You know."

When I say his name, J.J. looks me in the eye once more. "You told me not to get involved with him. You could've—and should've—washed your hands of me and walked away."

We're so close. Have we been this close, face to face, before? Not on opposite sides of the Block, with the street and cruising cars vying for our attention. Not when groups of working boys would congregate for food at one of the Grace Street after hours spots. Not even those nights when he would spoon me from behind so I wouldn't feel alone.

His eyes are so clear, so sweet. They dance over my features, taking in every detail. "I don't like saying *I told you so*," he murmurs, as we stare at each other. "And you're not going to hear me say it..."

I grin. "But..."

"But I did." He's still laughing when I reach out and press my palms against the light beard on his cheeks. I pull J.J.'s face to mine, tilt my head, and kiss him.

He responds instantly, hungrily, by closing what

distance remains between us and pulling me tight. Strong arms wrap around my body; fingertips dig into my shoulders, my back, my butt. I had been the initial aggressor, but his own instincts rev from zero to a hundred in seconds. I scarcely notice when he tosses me onto my new bed.

My excitement grows as he struggles out of his sweater and tank top to reveal that strong, deep chest I'd always admired. Then we're kissing again, his tongue probing as deeply as it can go. I respond by welcoming him, by wrapping my legs and arms around the strong trunk of his body, with my gasps, with my sighs. This act is what I've saved for myself. For someone important.

It's worth it.

That flowery scent again. So sweet, utterly J.J.— delicate as a June Sunday. I pull away from the passionate embrace to bury my face in his chest just to smell it. The hair there grows thick; it grazes my smooth skin. When my tongue flicks against his nipple, and he chokes with gratification, I know what to do next. I plant my lips on that flat, dark disc and suck. He sighs and watches me work, exclaiming when I scrape my teeth over the sensitive flesh. Through his jeans, I can feel his erection, rigid against my abs. The harder I suck, the more I nibble and gently bite, the more insistent it becomes. My lips and teeth fix upon his other nipple. Since he enjoys the attention, my fingers manipulate the wet nub I have to neglect.

We can't stay cooped up in these clothes for much longer. There's a moment in which we simply look at the other, nod, and leap up to shuck everything we're wearing. Garments fly everywhere, hitting the linoleum at random. Then we're savaging each other again. The box springs squeak and strain as we writhe, hips gyrating on hips. Our dicks want to merge into one, it seems; we're grinding them with such determination.

His mouth covers mine. My hands grasp his ass, the small of his back, the back of his head. His fingers wrap around my cock and squeeze, hard. When they rub against the outside of my hole, instinctively my legs part. If that's what J.J. wants, that's what J.J. will get. But no: his ministrations there are only fleeting. Next thing I know, he's shifting positions. He kneels over me, ass almost touching the headboard, so that I'm staring up at his dick. His eyes bore downwards into mine. "I want my Buttercup's lips on me," he whispers.

Never has that nickname sounded sexier.

I've never seen his dick before. I'm staring at it up close now. It's a massive, meaty thing. A solid nine, at the very least, at least six inches around, with a distinct curve to his left. J.J.'s so excited that the hood of his foreskin has retracted, though luxurious folds gather around the ridge. "Oh, fuck," I say, intimidated by the heft of the thing.

He extends himself with his fingers, pointing that colossus toward my mouth. "Maybe later." Despite his serious face, I know he's teasing. "I want that pretty mouth, first, Nicky. You gonna suck it real good?"

"Yes, sir," I promise, with a nod. I open wide to receive him.

I know I'm in for a challenge when I have to drop my jaw like a python to take him. My mouth is full, and there's still more to follow; I'm close to choking when, finally, my nose presses into his spicy-scented balls. My throat is already sore. My neck aches. Involuntary tears stream from the corners of my eyes. Still, I am the happiest I've been in a very long time.

Once again, his position shifts as he lowers himself on me. I feel wetness around my own cock as his mouth engulfs me. I can't protest—only suck harder. Normally, I'm not into sixty-nining. It's uncomfortable. It feels like a lot of work for little reward. It's too much sensation. Right now, though, with this handsome man who's helping me break in my new bed, none of those apply. I want all the sensation, and I want it now.

I lose myself in what follows, though instinct keeps me deep-throating my friend's enormous tool. His thighs surround my ears, so the sounds of our enjoyment arrive muffled, as if from underwater. Some of them are my own. I only know I want to feast forever at his buffet.

When I feel the warning signs from the base of my cock, I attempt to protest—to warn him to slow down. That's impossible, though, when my throat is being so thoroughly sodomized. Bolts of electricity shoot from my cock and along my spine, forcing my hips upward.

J.J. notices. Instead of backing off, he redoubles his efforts. Around my shaft his fingers wrap; his tongue slithers around my pole to bring it over the edge. Lightning flashes before my closed eyes, then an eruption of lava. I'm shooting deep into my buddy's mouth while he slurps and swallows every drop. My excitement feeds into his. Before I know it, his already substantial girth stretches my lips out even further. A salty promise of what's to come coats my tonsils.

Then, without warning—or perhaps I simply can't hear it, with his legs squeezing my skull with such determination—comes the flood. Gush after gush of semen fills my cheeks and spills down my chin. Between thrusts, I gulp down as much as I'm able. By the time he pulls out, though, I'm a soggy and sticky mess. With my red, cum-spattered face, I must look as if I've been sucking an entire football team. All that semen is from one dick, though. And I've never been more content.

It's with surprising tenderness that J.J. wipes his residue from my cheeks and chin. He strokes my hair and brushes it back into place with his soft fingers, looks me in the eyes to make sure I'm okay. Then he kisses me on the forehead. I snuggle up to him, inhaling that familiar June scent. In his embrace, I feel less like a big dumb ox and more like a small thing, tiny enough to be taken care of, delicate enough to merit protection. I like the novelty of it.

"Damn, Buttercup. How come we didn't do this before?" he chuckles sleepily as he caresses the back of my neck. His eyes are closed.

Mine, though, remain wide open. There's a single drop of semen beading his dick, round and creamy as a pearl. "Honeysuckle," I say, finally recognizing what's been eluding me. "You smell like honeysuckle."

"I beg your pardon?"

I laugh a little at his rebuke. "When you were a kid, did you ever try to get honey from a honeysuckle blossom?" He shakes his head. "Never? For real? Okay, when honeysuckle blooms, you pluck a blossom from the vine. You grab the little knob where it connected, tug down, and it drags down this thing called the stigma through the tube at the bottom. It looks like a skinny cock with a big head."

"Is that the kind of botany they taught you back home?" J.J.'s chest rumbles with amusement. "Go on."

"As it drags through the honeysuckle tube, the head collects nectar. Just a tiny, tiny drop. Ready for the tip of your tongue." My finger scoops the pearl from his dick. I show it to him, then lick it off with a smack.

"Does it taste like honey?" he wants to know.

My nose wrinkles. "It does. A little drop of summer sweetness, right in your own back yard."

"Honeysuckle," J.J.'s murmur sounds distant, but he pulls me close. "Kinda crazy, the lengths someone will go for a taste of sweetness." He pulls me even closer to share a deep kiss. My mouth responds to his, eager for more. "I'll give you all the honey you can stand," he promises in a diminishing voice, before drifting off.

I wrap my arms around my slumbering lover and assure myself it will not be for the last time.

HUSTLER'S LUCK

A Short Story
by Adam Maxwell Bigglesworth

HUSTLER'S LUCK

Frankie hustled to pay the rent. He accepted money from gentlemen in exchange for sex. It's the oldest profession. Perhaps in the days of cavemen, the fairer sex traded her pussy for a leg of bison. Young boys plied their asses for protection from the older, more dangerous males. When currency came on the scene, the nature of the business changed from pure barter to a proxy by money. But the industry itself has never changed. Horny men want sex and are willing to do anything to get it. Beautiful men and women can sell their beauty to the highest bidder. That was Frankie's line of work.

Frankie initially approached hustling with a modicum of fear and shame. He knew that the roughest trade sold their greatest commodity: a big dick in the ass of their clients. Frankie was at the opposite end. He had almost no dick, but his ass was very accommodating. His clientele were not the rich pansies from Beverly Hills. He attracted the men on the down low, macho men who craved a little tenderness and a boy's hole to fuck. On some days, it felt like hard work. He didn't mind the fucking, but he hated the body odor, bad breath, pimples, rolls of fat, cigars, and all the other unpleasant macho trappings that came with the sex. He tried to focus on whatever made a client attractive. Maybe they were handsome or muscular. Their teeth were perfect, even if they were overweight. He didn't need to perform beyond accepting a cock in his hole and pretending to like it.

The rough trade with their big dicks had to work much harder to stay hard when they were with an unattractive client. Frankie heard them complain all the time.

Brian, a pimply hustler with a plump cock said, "Fucking faggot looked like a rat with no fur. I had to snort two lines of speed just to get it up!"

His running buddy, Grover, said, "My trick last night had a booger in his nose, and he only smiled when I asked him to wipe it. I thought I was gonna puke."

Brian turned to Frankie. "You got it easy. You just lay back and let them do all the work. I'll bet they don't even care if you get hard."

Frankie shrugged. "If it's so easy, why don't you do it?"

Brian growled under his breath, and Grover chuckled. Frankie knew he was right. None of them would get paid if the work wasn't a chore. Sexy men and pretty boys never paid for sex. That's not how it works. Frankie had yet to find an exception until tonight.

At ten o'clock, a black Mercedes convertible rolled up to the curb and stopped in front of Frankie. Brian and Grover stepped forward, but when the window rolled down, they knew it wasn't for them.

The man behind the window was pure muscle, with tufts of hair sprouting from his chest. He wore thick horn-rimmed glasses that accentuated his green eyes. His closely cropped hair was slicked back so it shone in the street lamp's light.

"How much?" He smiled at Frankie with a perfect set of white teeth. This guy checked all the boxes. Frankie's heart skipped a beat when he caught a whiff of the man's cologne mixed with his aromatic sweat. It wasn't body odor; it was pure sex.

Frankie knew there had to be a catch. "Are you a cop?"

The man laughed. "No, of course not."

Frankie put one hand on his slender hip. "What is a guy like you doing looking to pay for sex? You look like you could have your choice of men."

The john smiled. "Looks can be deceiving. Tell me, how experienced are you? You been with a lot of guys?"

Frankie sneered. "I'm a whore; what do you think?"

The guy held up both hands. "I only ask because I need someone with experience. I have a, uh, unique problem."

Frankie switched hips. The handsome trick had piqued his curiosity. "Go on."

The big brute motioned Frankie to the window. "Take a look."

Frankie looked where the man's hand landed in his lap. He wore tan trousers, which showed the outline of an ungodly huge cock. Frankie gasped. He realized he couldn't see all of it. There was so much dick that it just disappeared in the darkness.

The man said, "If you don't want to go through with it, I'll understand."

Grover stepped forward and put a hand on Frankie's shoulder. "What's up? Is this guy bothering you?"

Frankie shook his head and pointed. Grover said, "Holy shit! Dude! That ain't natural."

The john rolled his eyes. "You think I haven't heard that before? Buzz off; this is between me and him."

Frankie shooed Grover away. "I got this; back off."

The man smiled. "So you never answered. How much?"

Frankie sighed. "Are you gonna fuck me with that?"

The man shrugged. "I'd like to try. Like I said, no big deal if you can't handle it."

Frankie bristled. He didn't like it when people underestimated him. He had no idea if he could handle it.

"Okay, look. If I can't handle it, you just pay twenty-five and drop me off back here. If I can, it's two hundred."

The man smiled. "That's all?"

Frankie cursed under his breath. He should have known a guy with a car like his would be rich. "Get in, and we'll see where it goes."

⚜

THE CAR HEADED AWAY FROM THE BOULEVARD into the West Hollywood Hills on Sunset Plaza Drive. This neighborhood was where the richest homos lived. The car turned off before Mulholland onto a side street that turned out to be a wide drive-way. They pulled up to an automatic gate, which opened on its own.

Frankie asked, "How did you do that?"

The muscle-bound hunk shrugged. "My butler got notified when we turned up the drive."

Butler? Frankie felt like he was in over his head. He hoped the guy didn't expect him to be well-hung. He would be sorely disappointed.

"You can call me Ralph, by the way. What's your name?"

"Frankie."

As the car pulled up to a spectacular mansion, they shook hands. When Ralph exited the car, Frankie saw the full length of the thick, long cock, nearly to the knee.

Ralph saw Frankie's terrified face. "I don't expect a miracle. You can always fuck me if it doesn't work out. I'm used to it."

There it was. Frankie groaned inwardly. Ralph saw his reaction.

"What, did I say something wrong?"

Frankie shook his head. "You'll see soon enough."

Ralph frowned. "You got the opposite problem, don't you?"

Frankie shrugged. "Yeah."

Ralph smiled. "Twenty-five bucks unless you can pull off a miracle. I'm getting away cheap tonight."

Frankie said, "Yeah, but if I can take it, make it five hundred. I hadn't seen the whole thing."

Ralph laughed. "Fair enough. Come inside."

The inside of the mansion looked like a palace. Ornate gold sconces and crystal chandeliers lit the entrance hall. Antique furniture that looked like it had been stolen from European royalty filled the living room.

"Have a seat."

Frankie sank into a settee from the 1700s.

Ralph opened a cabinet filled with liquor. "What do you drink?"

"Rum and Coke. Easy on the rum." Frankie didn't like to drink on the job. You never knew when things could turn ugly.

Ralph clinked glasses with Frankie. "To a night of mystery."

Frankie smiled and took a sip. It was the smoothest rum he'd ever tasted.

Ralph said, "You like it? It's Barbados Estate. Best in the world."

Frankie was dying of curiosity. "How did you get all this money?"

Ralph smiled. "I sell nuclear secrets to the Russians." He laughed heartily. "Kidding. I produce films."

"Have I seen any of them?"

Ralph shrugged. "Probably. Sci-Fi, Horror, Adventure. You've likely seen quite a few."

Frankie said, "I don't think I'll ever be rich."

Ralph leaned forward. "Let me tell you a secret. When I got to Hollywood, all I had was this dick. I used to do what you do before I invested in my first film."

"Did you fuck guys?"

Ralph shook his head. "I lured them in with this." he squeezed his cock mid-thigh, "but nobody ever let me fuck them. I'm still a virgin in that respect. A few of the pansies liked to fuck my ass."

Frankie said, "Yeah, I never fucked anyone either. Can't."

Ralph said, let me see.

Frankie pulled down his jeans, revealing the tiny clit of a cock between his legs.

"Does it grow?"

Frankie shook his head.

"We're more alike than it would appear, eh, kid?"

He leaned forward, putting his mouth on Frankie's tiny penis, licking it like a man eating a pussy.

Frankie started in surprise. No trick had ever tried that.

Ralph said, "So beautiful. Your face, your little penis, your narrow waist. You know you're beautiful, right?"

"Shut up and keep doing that. It feels good."

Ralph went down again. Frankie put his hand on the close-cut hair and pressed. It felt great. He'd never known anything like it. Poor Ralph had probably never had a mouth on his cock, at least not around it. Maybe on it, like nibbling at the edge.

Ralph stopped. "I gotta get these pants off. I'm getting hard. I don't want to ruin them."

Frankie chuckled. He'd never heard of such a problem. He marveled as Ralph stood, unbuckling his belt. The thick cock had crept below his knee. Ralph struggled to pull the tight linen pants down. When he got them below his knee, the massive cock swung forward, framed by Ralph's hairy, muscular thighs. Frankie shuddered.

"That's my beast. I call him Ralph Senior." Ralph laughed at his own witty remark as he kicked off the pants. The cock was more than knee length. The head was the size and shape of a Granny Smith apple. The shaft was narrow below the head but grew very thick in the middle, perhaps as big around as a baby's head, then narrowed near the base. Frankie liked cocks shaped like that. They felt good when they were closer to a normal size. When the trick pulled out, it hurt a little; when he pushed back in, there was a little relief.

"Fuck, that's big."

Ralph grinned. "That's my money maker."

Frankie turned and bent to remove his jeans, revealing his plump ass. "And this is mine."

Ralph whistled. He knelt, tonguing Frankie's hole. "It's loose, but I don't think you're gonna be able to handle it."

Frankie whirled around. "Wanna bet?"

Ralph said, "Okay. It's free if you can't, or a thousand if you can."

Frankie needed that. It was nearly three months' rent. If it ripped him in two, it would still be worth it. "You're on."

Ralph said, "Let's go upstairs to my bed."

෴

THE BEDROOM LOOKED LIKE THE SET OF "Cleopatra." Gold tablets with hieroglyphics and Platinum sarcophagi lined the walls. One wall featured the same silk-lined settee in which Liz Taylor seduced Richard Burton. A massive round mattress, covered in silks and furs, dominated the center of the room. A mirrored ceiling reflected everything. Frankie was awestruck.

Ralph removed his white button-down, revealing

a thick, hairy, muscular chest. He held Frankie against it.

"Chew on it."

Frankie obeyed. The nipple was large and supple. He flicked it between his tongue and teeth.

"Harder."

Frankie bit down, and Ralph moaned. His cock lifted until it touched Frankie's tiny penis. Swiftly, Ralph lifted Frankie onto the settee, rolling him back to expose his hole. He picked up where he left off, forcing his strong tongue deep into Frankie's hole, loosening and lubricating it. Frankie loved when his tricks did this. He cleaned up every night before he left his flat just in case he got lucky. He was lucky tonight, but he feared his luck would end when Ralph finally got around to the fucking.

Ralph had high-end lube made to help cows give birth. That seemed appropriate, given the situation. Ralph laid a towel on the bed. This stuff was messy. He squirted some into his palm and wiped it on Frankie's hole. Then he inserted three fingers. Frankie was fine even at four, but it started to hurt when Ralph got his thumb in him and pushed.

"If I warm you up with my fist, you might be able to take a little."

Frankie agreed. There was so much lube inside him that he couldn't resist when Ralph pushed past his sphincter. It hurt like hell, but Frankie had no choice but to accept the hairy fist in his asshole.

Ralph looked surprised. "You're pretty good, son. That's a lot of fist you just took."

Frankie grinned. "A thousand bucks will loosen any boy's ass."

Ralph chuckled. "You'd be surprised how many give up."

Ralph pushed past his wrist until his muscled forearm painfully stretched Frankie open.

"Is it okay?"

Frankie nodded. "Keep going. I can take it."

Ralph made it up to the elbow before Frankie tapped out. He withdrew quickly, causing Frankie's hole to cramp. "Ow! Slowly."

Ralph apologized. He squirted some of the cow lube on his cock, but it wasn't enough. He did another long squirt and slicked it up. It shone in the light of the chandelier.

"You ready to disappoint me?" He sounded defeated already.

Frankie gave a wry smile. "I never disappoint. You'll learn that soon." He was all bravado and barely believed his own words.

Ralph positioned the throbbing head in front of Frankie's hole, which opened slightly in anticipation of the battering ram.

When Ralph pushed, Frankie saw stars. The room spun. He was in dire pain. He reached into his pocket and pulled out a vial of poppers. Sniffing deeply, he left the room for a minute. Ralph pressed in, and to his surprise, the tip went in halfway to the corona.

Frankie felt like he was giving birth. He pushed out like he was pooping, a trick he learned early in his career. The head slipped another half-inch. Frankie breathed in harsh gasps, struggling to put aside the pain. He took another deep whiff of the poppers, and his hole, slippery with lube, gave way.

With an audible pop, Ralph's head pushed past the sphincter.

"Holy fuck!" The muscular stud was visibly shocked that he had gotten this far. Frankie would have felt proud if he wasn't too busy processing the pain. He sniffed the poppers hard. The shaft was huge, but the baby's head was still to come. As Ralph pushed forward, the massive head of his cock struck the rectum wall.

Ralph sighed. "I guess that's as far as it goes." He started to pull back, but Frankie grabbed his leg.

"Wait, don't."

"I can't go any further."

Frankie winked. "But you can." He leaned to one side. "Go ahead."

Ralph pushed, striking the rectum wall again. But then he felt an opening. He pushed, and the tip of his head slipped past it.

"What's that? Did I rip a hole?"

Frankie laughed. "It's the second door. Go on through."

Ralph pushed. He was surprised at how easily his head slipped in. Frankie knew the nerves were different. They didn't have as many pain signals. His eyelids fluttered as Ralph moved through him. He looked down, surprised to see at least four inches of exposed flesh still waiting to enter him. He needed Ralph to keep going, or he'd pass out.

Frankie leaned forward, grabbed Ralph's ass, and pulled him close. The relief was intense.

Ralph looked at Frankie's tiny penis. "You're leaking."

Frankie nodded.

"It's hot."

"Yeah, you're doing that."

Ralph balked. "I haven't even started fucking you yet."

"It's the pressure. Keep going."

As the last inch of Ralph's cock entered him, the thickest part in the middle was forcing its way through the colorectal junction, or the "second door," as Frankie called it. He groaned in delight.

"Am I hurting you?"

"Shut up and fuck me."

Ralph pulled back slowly, a few inches, then pushed back in.

Frankie whined. "Harder!"

Ralph was astonished. He was definitely a thousand dollars down. He took shallow strokes, afraid to damage the kid's insides.

"Is that harder? Come on! Fuck my ass!"

Frankie watched in the mirrored ceiling as Ralph's muscular ass cheeks tightened with each forward lunge. The creamy white ass was a stark contrast to his honey-colored legs. It was hairless, unlike the furry thighs and shins. The sight of it was such a turn-on that Frankie swooned.

Inside an ass for the first time, Ralph felt a rush of emotion. His eyes welled up with tears. Frankie saw it. It was touching. He envied Ralph, who finally learned what it feels like to fuck someone. Frankie would never, ever know; he lacked the proper equipment.

Ralph kissed Frankie. "Thank you. You're a miracle."

Frankie knew he was good. Ralph's tremendous cock was easily three times as big as the biggest he'd ever had. He was awestruck by his sexual powers. They exceeded all expectations.

"You can take longer strokes. You've opened me up now."

Ralph pulled back a few inches more before driving it home. Frankie loved how his huge cock grew fatter and thinner as he moved through him. His little penis was drooling. In the mirror, he saw inch after inch exposed before they slipped back inside him. It was hot.

"Oh fuck, that's good. Keep going."

Ralph sped up a little, and his strokes grew longer. He pulled the middle part out at one point, and the head popped out of the second door. The double shot sent Frankie into spasms.

Ralph was concerned. "Are you okay?"

Frankie thrashed as Ralph pushed back in, filling him completely. "Oh, God! Oh, holy shit!"

Ralph was still worried. "Am I hurting you?"

Frankie was drowning in ecstasy. He managed to croak out a few words. "Don't stop. Fuck me."

Ralph slowed down, fearing what he might do to Frankie's guts. Frankie would have none of it. He grabbed Ralph's ass and pulled him in, then pushed him out, fast, hard. "Like that!"

Ralph shook his head, but he obeyed. Using his powerful hip muscles, he pounded into Frankie. His cock head rubbed back and forth through the second door, bringing him closer to orgasm. It caused Frankie to twitch and shake. His tiny soft penis grew hard. It throbbed like a hammer-struck thumb.

Ralph's forehead dripped with musky sweat. The scent drove Frankie wild. His little penis shot a bucket of cum onto his belly.

Ralph saw the hands-free ejaculation, and it sent him over the top.

"Oh god, I'm coming, too." Frankie felt a familiar warm flood in his guts, much deeper than he'd ever imagined possible. Ralph collapsed on top of him, shaking with orgasm. Frankie wrapped his arms and legs around the man, kissing him passionately. He couldn't love this man, his client, but his heart wanted to. It was more painful than the sex.

His eyes watered as he stared at Ralph's face.

"Hey, what are the tears?"

Frankie sniffed. "Nothing. I felt something real for a second."

Ralph said, "You did? I did, too."

Frankie inhaled the masculine aroma mixed with the smell of cum and sweat. He was so full of cock; he had never been so satisfied. The young hustler had another moment where the whole world seemed to sparkle. He was safe in the arms of this big brute.

Ralph pressed him. "What did you feel? Was it good?"

Frankie nodded. "It was. I felt safe."

Ralph hugged Frankie. "I want you to be safe. I-I don't know why. I just want you in my arms."

Frankie's cynicism kicked in. "You just want to fuck me again."

Ralph looked hurt. "Yeah, of course, but it's more than that."

Frankie was stunned. It was more. He was right. He was afraid it was the L word. But this man was in the clouds, so far above Frankie's lowly station in life. Love wasn't an option. It was commerce, plain and simple. "Did I earn my thousand dollars?"

Ralph grew cold. "Of course. Did you think I wouldn't pay?"

Frankie regretted his glib comments. "I'm sorry, Ralph. I'm not used to feeling this way. I'm scared."

"Me too."

They let that hang in the air. Frankie decided to go for broke. "I don't think I've ever been in love before."

Ralph smiled. "You feel it, too?"

They kissed. Frankie never returned to the Boulevard. He shared in Ralph's wealth but had to work for it every night. It was the best job he'd ever had.

THE FISH

by Peter Schutes

AN INNOCENT MAN

Fish. That's what they call me here. It means I'm brand new to prison life and don't have a clue what's going on. It's an accurate description. I know everyone in prison says they are innocent, but in my case, it's true. A horrible person, short and red-headed like me, is out there roaming free. They held up the liquor store by my house at gunpoint. They shot the owner in the leg. While this was happening, I was suffering a massive head cold. I walked down to the liquor store to get some DayQuil and found the owner unconscious and bleeding. I called 911 and stayed with him until the ambulance arrived.

Here are the mistakes I made. First, the asshole dropped the gun. I found it near the door and picked it up. I don't know why I did that. Second, the owner revived several times, and I slapped his face to wake him. He was so out of it; I think all he remembered was my face. He picked me out in a line-up after the police found my prints on the gun. My third and worst mistake was running when the cops tried to apprehend me. Let this be a warning to everyone reading this: if the cops are coming for you, let them. Be agreeable. Don't fight.

The fingerprints were circumstantial evidence, but the owner was an extremely credible eyewitness who pointed me out to the jury. Add to that my mad dash for freedom, and it was an open-and-shut case. Nobody bought my story then, so I don't expect you to buy it now. But it's true.

I spent time in the county jail, but they released me on bail because it was a first offense. After the trial, I was shepherded away in handcuffs. I got on a bus with a dozen other "innocent" prisoners, and we drove off to hell. The bus ride was the last peaceful moment before the chaos of prison. We all sat silently, facing our doom. Nobody looked at anyone else, and I just stared at my lap, desperately fighting off the tears threatening to fall from my eyes. Crying in prison is like an invitation to a beating for the predators that circle the yard, looking for weakness. Sobbing on the bus was probably dangerous, but it was hard not to control it. The tiny glimpse of prison life I got in the county jail was so wretched and cruel that I doubted I would survive. And I wouldn't have if it weren't for Mike Hawk.

MIKE HAWK

The guards marched us from the bus to an intake room, where a sleazy corrections officer watched us remove our clothes. He took extra care during the cavity search, whistling with admiration at a few of us whose rectums were to his liking. He smacked my bare bottom and said, "They're gonna eat you up, fish. Salmon supper tonight." "Salmon" was a reference to my red hair. It's really more Auburn.

What came next is now a bittersweet memory. At the time, it felt like my life was over. After the cavity search, we put on our prison garb. The officer handed us each a bundle with a blanket, toothbrush, toothpaste, a tiny towel, and a soap bar. We formed a line and marched to our cells. My cell was in the middle of a loud hallway, with cells facing each other. As I walked, hands reached out to grab my big ass, which has always been too big for a short man like me. The cries and jeers were cacophonous. I'm not afraid to admit I was the youngest, best-looking guy at Corcoran. The whoops and hollers weren't for anyone but me. The cell appeared empty because I hadn't seen Mike Hawk on the top bunk. As I un-packed my meager belongings, Mike whistled. It startled me.

"Holy shit, I caught a live one!" He jumped down to look me over. Grabbing me roughly by the shoulder, he said, "Turn around. I want to see what's for dessert."

I blushed and stood my ground. "I ain't your dessert, for fuck's sake."

Mike feigned an apology. "Oh, sorry, little man, my mistake."

The words "little man" stung. I was little everywhere except my massive butt. Many redheads are blessed between the legs, but I bore the 'Irish curse.' My two-inch cock hardly even qualified as a penis.

Mike rubbed his crotch. His cock showed huge, even through his baggy scrubs. I gulped. Yeah, I'm gay, but I never really liked big dicks. They made me feel inadequate. Mike's massive blessing was most unwelcome. I did admire his strong pectoral muscles, with thimble-sized nipples poking through his white t-shirt. He caught me eying his chest and flexed his pecs one at a time.

"Don't play hard to get, little man. I'm Mike. Mike Hawk. What's your name, Fish?"

I frowned. "Brandon Little."

Without asking, Mike put his hand down the front of my pants. "Shoo-wee, that's little alright."

When I turned bright red, he put a reassuring hand on my shoulder. "I dig the tiny ones. Seriously."

I felt a strange wave of relief. It was like I had been defending my smallness from the entire gay world, and here in prison, I found acceptance from my new, obnoxious cellmate.

We stared at each other. Mike continued to rub his crotch, and the monster inside his sweatpants swelled beyond normal proportions and then beyond the impossible. My asshole twitched with fear.

"You said you're not dessert, so let's make you an appetizer."

In one swift movement, Mike held my head against the cell wall. His cruel cock jutted from the fly of his scrubs. Roughly, he pulled down my scrubs, revealing my large, feminine ass.

"Oh shit, dude, I'm gonna cum just looking at your ass. Fuckin' beautiful!"

He spat into his hand and slicked it up. He knew he was too big, and he had some technique. He spat many times as he forced his way in. It started as non-consensual, but by the time he hit the end of my rectum, I was hooked.

"You like that, Smalls?"

I nodded.

"Ready for the rest?"

I couldn't believe there was more. Mike pushed in hard and suddenly went to a place I'd only heard about. He was in my colon. When it went in, I yelped. That didn't stop him. He fucked hard and fast. I moaned with unwanted pleasure. Before I knew it, he'd blasted my guts with cum. Then he kissed me. My heart fluttered. Maybe prison wouldn't be so bad after all.

THE AUCTION BLOCK

With Mike's cum still dripping from my ass, we walked to the cafeteria. I was his property, and he made it clear to anyone who so much as made eyes at me.

A big Latino with tattoos on his face smiled at me. "Wow, look at that ass!" Before he could finish whistling, Mike puffed up his muscles and stood between us. The big guy backed down. Mike was Nazi Lowrider (NLR). He didn't have beef with the Norteños or Sureños; they wanted to keep it that way. You can judge all you want, but racism in prison is just how the whole system works. If you're white, you'd better get with a white gang. It sucks. I don't feel incredibly proud of white culture. We invented colonialism, democracy, and banking, but that doesn't make us superior. And really, "white" isn't an ethnicity. Italians invented banking, Greeks invented democracy, and Colonialism was most of Europe. Africans built the pyramids, Asians built the Great Wall, and native Peruvians built Macchu Picchu. Who's to say any one race is superior? I certainly don't. But tell that to men who commit crimes and spend their lives around other territorial men. I promise you they don't listen.

Mike turned to me. "Stay close to me. You can't trust any of these motherfuckers."

I felt a weird mixture of shame and excitement at being protected by Mike Hawk. He was a perfect specimen of toxic masculinity. He must spend six hours a day lifting weights in the yard. Every muscle, every sinew rippled as he moved. Unlike Mike, the mighty oak tree, I was a little leaf blowing in the wind.

"Dinner," if you could call it that, was reconstituted mashed potatoes, grey cabbage, a slice of white bread, and a piece of mystery meat floating in corn starch and water. Mike and I sat with his white supremacist mates at the white table. The guys all checked my ass out. Some of them were incredibly hot. They wore bandanas to shield their eyes, so it was hard to tell where they were looking. But I knew when they were staring at my big bubble butt because they'd drool a little. I quickly realized that Mike wasn't just protecting me. He was pimping me out.

A tall, lanky blond with a swastika on his neck looked me over. "I'll give you ten smokes."

Mike balked. "Ten? Fuck, Wade, that ass is worth two cartons!"

Wade shook his head. "One pack."

"One carton!" Mike didn't even look my way. I was a commodity to be bartered, not a human being.

"Three packs. That's half my stash, bro."

Mike sighed. "Alright, but you only get one hour."

Wade snorted. "I need at least two."

Mike waved his hand. "Fine."

I said, "Uh, excuse me. What is this?"

Mike smacked me hard across the face. "Shut up, bitch. Speak when you're spoken to, got it?"

My cheek stung. I put a hand over it. It felt hot. I hadn't really noticed anything about Wade but his Nazi tattoo. I got a closer look at his goatee. It was a mix of red and blond hair, like strawberry blond. His eyes were dark green. He scratched his crotch through his sweatpants. He knew I was checking him out. What I saw worried me. His soft cock showed through the sweats as he scratched. It reached down his thigh toward his knee. Soft, it was longer than Mike's. Hopefully, he wasn't a grower.

A short, squat cholo-looking dude with bronzed skin and a brown crew cut was next.

"Homes, I need some ass bad."

Mike said, "Half a carton, Gino.."

Gino balked. "It's three packs, and you know it."

Mike smiled. "You know your fat dick is gonna put wear and tear on the merchandise."

I looked at the crotch of his sweatpants. There was a massive chunk of meat in there. It didn't go down one leg or the other, but it created a pillow-like effect.

Gino said, "I can't help if I'm hung fatter'n you."

Mike said, "Wait, you smoke menthols. No deal"

"Nah, I'll get you Marlboro Red."

Mike said, "You got funds?"

Gino said, "Yeah, my old lady deposited last week."

"Throw in some Fritos to clever any damage, and you got a deal."

Gino thought for a few seconds. "Yeah, man, that's cool."

I shifted nervously, loathing the feeling of being a slave on the auction block.

Mike continued to enlist his gang members in this pile-on of sexual commerce. I'd never felt so powerless. But underneath the dread, I felt a strange, guilty sense of anticipation.

HOW I LOST MY VIRGINITY

My ass was going to take a beating, but I always wanted to be used like this. It was a secret fantasy that started in high school when the thugs took an interest in me, knowing I was a homo. I lost my virginity senior year to Dwayne Paulson.

Dwayne was a bully, my bully, and he'd made my life hell for four years. Then one day, he started being nice to me. I'm ashamed to say it felt nice being shown friendship after so many years of torture. I guess I had Stockholm Syndrome.

Dwayne began showing more than friendship. We lived near each other. Whereas in the past, I used to run home so he wouldn't beat the shit out of me, now I was walking beside him.

One day walking home, he pushed me into an alleyway. His breath got heavy.

He said, "Dude, I wanna suck your dick."

He'd never seen it. I had explicitly asked the Vice Principal to ensure we were never in the same gym class. He was happy to oblige.

I turned red. I wanted sex, but not like that. I said, "If you can find it."

Dwayne frowned. "What do you mean?"

I unzipped my pants and showed him the little nub.

"It doesn't grow any?"

I shook my head.

"Well then, why don't you suck mine?"

His was maybe four inches long and skinny, but it was big enough to suck. We got between two dumpsters, and I sucked him off. He came immediately.

"Damn, Brandon, that was fuckin' great!"

After that, it became a regular gig. We walked to and from school, and I gave Dwayne two blow jobs a day. Then he wanted more.

I had a bigger house than Dwayne with a full basement, which was rare in California. My folks had turned it into a den. There were tattered sofas, a TV, and a little half bathroom.

It was Senior Spring, unseasonably hot. Dwaune was covered in sweat when I stepped into the alleyway. He shook his head.

"I wanna watch TV in your basement." The way he said it, I knew it meant something else. He came from a poor family, and watching cable was probably a luxury for him, but the tone of his voice was strange. He had a dangerous gleam in his eye. I knew I was about to experience something new. My little dick dripped juice the whole way home.

In the downstairs den, Dwayne pushed me onto the sofa and lay on top of me. He pulled my shirt off, licking my nipples. They got hard, which surprised me.

"Fuck, dude, you got bitch tits."

It was true. I guess I had too much estrogen during puberty. I had saggy man boobs at eighteen. Dwayne kept licking them while he pulled off my pants. I instinctively put a hand over my crotch to hide my shame.

Dwayne shook his head. "Let me lick it."

It wasn't much bigger than a clit, and he apparently had eaten pussy at some point because he knew exactly what to do. I moaned like a girl, incredulous that anyone would want to put their mouth there. The pleasure outweighed the shame. I let him lick and tickle me until I was close to coming.

"Dwayne, I'm close."

He pulled back. "Don't come on my face."

It was too late. I splattered my former tormentor with more cum than I ever imagined possible. The look on Dwayne's face was terrifying.

"You dirty motherfucker. I told you not to come on me!"

He ran to the little half bath and washed his face. He used toilet paper to daub his t-shirt, which was stained wet. When he came back to the couch, his face had softened. He held my head and gave me my first kiss. With my pants around my ankles, Dwayne flipped me over so I was face down. He put his face in my crack and licked my hole. I wasn't prepared for it to feel so good. I had just blown my load, and I had that cold feeling you get after orgasm. At first, I was mad that he was continuing, but I liked it once he went to town on my ass. I got hard again.

He spat on his dick and pressed it into me. My big ass cheeks were in the way, so I spread them apart. Dwayne slipped in easily. His puny dick was just the right size for a virgin.

"Does it hurt?" Dwayne was almost tender when he asked.

I shook my head. "It feels good."

"That's what all the girls say."

Even with my cheeks spread, it wasn't enough for him to stay in.

He roughly flipped me over and held my legs over my head. With jeans around my ankles, I couldn't open them. He impatiently threw my shoes in the corner and helped me off with my jeans. On my back, with my ass on the hard pillows, he had a straight shot to my hole. He held my cheeks apart and licked my twitching, puckered asshole. He spat on his cock and shoved it in. This time it hurt a little, but it faded immediately. His little mushroom head rubbed against my prostate. I leaked pre-cum into his pubic hair.

"Damn, Brandon, you're dripping like a bitch."

I didn't care what he said. His little dick was taking me to paradise. He leaned over and kissed me, and his dick slipped out. He put it back in, grinding his hips since he couldn't pump them without falling out.

"You like that?" His lips were red from kissing me so hard.

I nodded. I did. I fucking loved it!

He held my ass aloft and put a couch cushion under it. In that position, he could slide back and forth just enough to fuck. He got rough. I wanted it rougher.

"Harder!"

Dwayne didn't need encouragement. He pounded shallowly but hard. The saliva was drying out, and my asshole burned and ached. But Dwayne didn't have much staying power. He grunted like a hog.

"Fuck, oh shit. Oh, shit!" And just like that, he released a fertile flood of cum into my aching hole.

After that, it became a daily ritual. Twice daily on weekends. My parents were just glad I'd "found a friend." They had no idea what went on in that basement. I never grew tired of it, but Dwayne did. When summer came around, we fucked twice a day. Neither of us were going off to college. But Dwayne met a chick and dumped me. He'd show up at my house once or twice a week, but only to fuck and split. I wanted more, so I left our two-horse town for a bigger city, Sacramento, And just like that, our bizarre fuck buddy relationship ended.

BITCH TWITCH

I may have taken twenty minutes to tell you the saga of Dwayne, but the whole memory passed through my mind in a few seconds. I came out of my reverie when Mike put a controlling hand on my neck and walked me to the next table, the Aryan Brotherhood (AB). They were a frightening white supremacist gang with a corner on the speed market in prison. You could feel the tension bristle when we approached.

The leader, appropriately named "Whitey," stepped forward. "Mike Hawk, how's my cock?"

"Fuck you, Whitey." It was a friendly exchange despite the harsh words.

"Who's the fish?

"This is Brandon Little, but you can call him "Smalls" if you know what I mean.

Whitey chuckled. "If he stands to pee, not for me. That goes for the whole Aryan Brotherhood, and you know it."

"Man, fuck your celibate bullshit; you know you want some."

Whitey folded his arms. "I'll think about it. We

make exceptions." Whitey pointed at me. Turn around!"

I rolled my eyes and slowly rotated, revealing my fat ass.

Whitey whistled. "Fuck, Mike, why you gotta start evil?"

A few drug deals later, I was scheduled for eleven ass fuckings and seven blow jobs; Mike was the wealthiest man in prison.

"You're a fucking goldmine, Smalls." I hated my new nickname. "Don't worry; you get to share in the wealth." Great, I could eat some fucking Fritos for free. Lucky I liked getting fucked so much. Dinner was over, and I had to return to the cell with my greedy pimp. He wanted more. I didn't care. I found a strange serenity in submitting to my captor. It was like nothing really mattered anymore. I said it before, but I felt like Br'er Rabbit in the sticker bush. Mike was kind as long as I pretended to be scared and unhappy. If I let him know what a slut I was, he'd probably mistreat me worse than he'd already done.

I was all loosened up from earlier, so the sex was even better. I was sore as shit, but my sphincter didn't put up a fight. Mike noticed.

"Are you getting loose already?" He smacked my ass hard, and I clenched involuntarily. "That's better."

Mike was a good lover, I was surprised to admit. He reminded me of Dwayne in so many ways. My hot cellmate planted kisses all over my body. Because he was so huge, he could kiss in places Dwayne had never dared. Every few minutes, he interrupted the kisses to smack my ass.

"Keep it tight, Smalls!"

The fifth or sixth smack had a strange effect. I started to shake. My abs clenched involuntarily and wouldn't stop.

Mike smiled. "You got bitch twitch. Man, those guys are gonna love fucking you!"

As my belly contracted, I could make out the outline of Mike's monster sliding through me like a snake under a blanket. No, not a mere snake, an Anaconda.

When he came, I shot my load. I barely had to touch myself.

"Now make my fucking bed, bitch." His pillow talk left a lot to be desired.

CORN HUSKERS LOTION
AND WADE

At breakfast - reconstituted eggs, spam gravy, and a sawdust biscuit, Wade sat down across from us, eying me like a tiger eyes a rabbit. His blond hair was combed back, revealing more racist tattoos on his scalp. He handed Mike three packs of Marlboro red. Mike tucked them in his waistband. Wade lifted his head in a quick salute. I was sold downriver.

After dropping my tray at the window, I felt a strong hand, rougher than Mike's, steering me by the neck. "Come on, Fish."

Wade guided me roughly to the laundry room. There was a broom closet. A laundry worker stood guard. Wade tipped him a cigarette, and the guy let us in. It smelled like thirty years' worth of sperm. It reminded me of a washroom with an attendant. From a hollowed-out br;ush, Wade fished out a condom.

"I ain't raw-dogging it with a faggot."

Behind a bottle of Formula 409 was a bottle of Corn Huskers lotion. Wade roughly pulled down my sweats and laughed. "You fuck with that?"

I shook my head, feeling smaller than my dick.

Wade shrugged and dropped his sweats. His cock hung to his mid-thigh, swelling. It didn't get very thick but was longer than Mike's. My ass twitched looking at it.

"Don't worry, man. If you can take Mike, you can take just about anyone except the fuckin'--" he said a racist slur too ugly to say out loud.

To my astonishment, a hose with a douche nozzle was attached to the sink. Wade roughly spat on it and inserted it in my butt. He turned on the cold water and filled me until I cramped.

Wade greased up my hole with the watery lotion. He tore open the condom with his teeth and rolled it a little more than halfway down his shaft before it ran out of length. He bent me over a stool and handed me the mop bucket for support.

True to his word, Wade slipped in easily, sliding to the back of my rectum in one smooth motion. He slid back and forth, slowly, gradually gaining speed. As he tapped my rectum, I felt an uncomfortable pressure against my bladder. Wanting to avoid pissing on the filthy floor, I twisted, letting him enter my colon.

"Holy shit!" Wade was surprised. "What did you do?"

"I guess you don't get much ass."

He punched my jaw from behind. I saw stars, but they cleared up. With a whole new chamber to explore, Wade took long, cruel strokes. The cornhusker's lotion was not a long-lasting lube. Wade spit on the condom, which helped a little. I shook a little, then the "bitch twitch" started up.

Wade whistled. "Damn, you know how to get fucked, don't ya, faggot?"

I groaned. "It's Smalls, please."

Wade chuckled. "Don't talk back." But he let my transgression slide. He was too amazed at the sensation of my insides stroking him in peristaltic waves.

My waist and hips bucked like a rodeo bull. I had no power to stop the cramping and squeezing deep in my belly.

Wade said, "Damn, boy. I usually take an hour. You're gonna get me off in fifteen minutes if you keep this up."

I knew better than to answer back. I moaned like a bitch in a porn film, which excited Wade even more. He kicked it up a notch, taking long, long strokes that dragged his head to the exit and back. The ring of his head was so wide it kept him from popping out. But I was getting looser and more relaxed. On one outstroke, he slipped out.

He popped his cock back inside me, then, Bam! He smacked me across the ass. I clenched, holding him in. He continued to spank me until there was a tap at the door.

The lookout said, "Dude, keep it down! Someone's gonna hear that."

Wade cursed under his breath and adjusted his fucking so that the widest part of his fat mushroom head squeezed my prostate repeatedly. I came like a woman, oozing ounce after ounce of pre-jizz on my thigh. It stuck to Wade's pubic hair. I hoped he wouldn't notice that I was getting him messy.

He was too far gone in bliss to notice anything. He bit his lower lip, grunting on each in-stroke and sucking air on the instroke. He was close. His hips became a blur as he fucked me senseless. I came in and out of consciousness, kneck deep in full body orgasm. I quivered and quaked like a leaf in the wind as the tall, dominant gangster drove me closer and closer to heaven.

"Oh fuck, you're better'n a bitch!"

Wade sped up faster than I ever thought possible. I stifled a cry, biting my clenched fist to hold back the moans. Then all at once, it stopped. I felt the long, powerful rod throb like a bee stinger. I saw his balls draw up close. His cock released a massive load of cum deep in my colon. He held his hips close to my thighs, emptying himself inside me for what seemed like a full minute.

"Yeah! Yeah! Oh fuck, yeah!" He wrapped his hands around my throat, cutting off my oxygen. Without warning, my minuscule penis shot a giant load of cum on Wade's belly.

"Fuckin' hands-free. Oh shit, you're a slut for cock, aren't you? You love to get fucked! I'm signing up for more, assuming you ain't wrecked the next time."

He hoisted me by the waist to a standing position. "Pull up your sweats."

I obeyed. Wade marched me back to Gen Pop, where Gino sat. His eyes widened in surprise.

"Back so soon? No good, eh?"

Wade winked. "Too good."

REACHING ACROSS THE AISLE

That night, Mike fucked me again. I preferred Wade's relatively thin cock, but Mike said he was "doing me a service" because Gino's fat cock, though average in length, was bigger around than his Anaconda.

I was getting used to Mike. I had never been with someone as big as him, but I was starting to like it. I did my best not to let it show. I had a feeling that if he knew I wanted it, he would use me more and more, and I would end up with a loose, flappy asshole.

Mike started by licking my ass. "You taste like cum. Didn't you wash out after?"

I shook my head.

"It's okay; it tastes kinda good. Don't tell Wade I said so."

We both laughed. I tried to picture Mike taking Wade's cock down his throat. Mike was such a dominant top it seemed impossible.

He started out gentle but pounded me hard once I relaxed and stopped wincing. I felt a guilty sense of attachment to my prison pimp. As he fucked me hard, I felt his massive presence in my gut; it was good. He was a terrible person but a fantastic lover. I understood why so many lovers stay together just because of the mind-blowing sex. When he reached a particular frequency of fucking I got the bitch twitch.

"Yeah, that's what I'm talking about. I'll bet no one else can do that to you."

I didn't dare tell him the truth: Wade had done it, too. I shook my head. "Only you."

His sweat fell like rain from his hair and brow onto my face and neck. I caressed his sweaty chest, holding my hand to my nose and breathing the heady aroma. It felt like I had just done poppers. His pheromones were turned up to eleven.

He stopped his fucking, letting my insides do all the work as they spasmed and stroked his magnificent cock. My eyes fluttered. He groaned, unleashed his baby gravy into my colon, and then collapsed on top of me. I tried to kiss him, but he rolled off and pulled his softening cock out of me, hand over hand, and kicked me out of his bed.

"Treat Gino right, Smalls. He needs it bad."

The following day at breakfast, I walked with a limp. Mike's vigorous fucking had worn me out. I could feel the lips of my ass rub against my cheeks. He had "turned me out."

The head of the Sureños approached the Nazi Lowrider table.

Mike stood, hands on his hips. "What you want, Luis?"

Luis looked like the cholos in my school. He'd cut the sweatpants into shorts. His long white socks were pulled up to his knees. I saw a big sausage in

there, swinging from side to side as he walked towards us.

"Listen, hombre. I seen you got merchandise for
sale. We want a cut of the action."

Mike shook his head. "He's booked for a few
weeks. Whites got priority."

Luis said, "We got dope, and you know it. Our
shit is the best tar you can score in here. Don't you
want to get high, ese? That Aryan Brotherhood shit
is nasty."

Mike shrugged. "How much will you give me for
a go at Smalls?"

Luis said, "An eighth of a gram. But, dude, it's
strong. Any more, and you would OD."

Mike laughed. "You know I don't do that shit,
Luis. I'll sell it to some lowlife, maybe someone in
your gang who doesn't want poontang."

Luis shrugged. "You can do whatever you want
with it; I don't give a shit."

Wade stepped forward. "Watch it, Luis. Don't
use curse words when you talk to the Lowriders."

Mike put a hand on Wade's shoulder. "It's okay,
man. At least he speaks English."

Luis bristled but didn't say anything. "We got a
truce, and I didn't mean no disrespect. I'm just
saying you can sell it, shoot it, smoke it, whatever
floats your boat."

Mike said, "A quarter gram in advance, and you
got yourself a deal. But it's more than two weeks
from now."

Luis reached into his waistband before shaking
Mike's hand. I saw two small balloons pass between
them.

Luis turned to leave, then looked over his shoulder. "You better keep your end of the bargain."

Mike nodded. Luis sauntered off, walking like one leg was longer than the other in a bounce step. I could tell he had a hard-on just thinking about me.

Mike spoke with the confidence of a coach. "Don't worry. They tell me he ain't a grower, and he comes real fast. He'll be an easy lay."

I groaned inwardly but plastered a smile on my face. "Great."

GINO'S TOO BIG

Gino shuffled up, holding his crotch, which looked like two softballs and a big can of tomatoes in his hands. "Dude, I got blue balls. Can we get a move on?"

Mike said, "Let the poor boy eat his breakfast."

Breakfast was shit on a shingle. Spam chunks in slimy gravy poured over stale white toast. It was the best meal they had in prison, and it was garbage. I had to hold my breath to eat it.

Down in the broom closet, Gino was all business. When he pulled his shorts down, I gasped. His cock was still growing, and it was already big around as a loaf of bologna. It didn't get any longer, but it kept getting fatter. There was no way I would be able to take him. He didn't bother with a condom. I doubt he would ever find one to fit anyway. He nodded toward the sink. I washed my hole until it ran clear.

Instead of Corn Huskers lotion, he dipped his hand in a greasy tub of waterless hand cleanser. I could smell the chemicals. There was no way that could be safe.

Gino read my mind. "It burns at first, but then

you'll be numb. Trust me, you want this in your ass." He spat on his cock several times, rubbing it in a circular motion until it glistened.

"I gotta start out in missionary; strip and lie on the floor."

The floor smelled like a Greyhound bus bathroom. I was so used to horrible smells in prison that it didn't even bother me. I was going to need a shower.

Gino bent my legs and pushed my knees to my ears. He whistled.

"Oh fuck, I never seen an ass so sweet." He walked forward on his knees until his basketball-sized cock head was pressed against my hole. He pushed, but nothing happened.

"Loosen up, mother fucker. Let me in."

I spread my cheeks apart and tried to think of something else. I thought about Dwayne, my high school tormentor. I thought about Mike Hawk, who was damn thick. I thought about taking a shit and pushed out. The first half-inch of Gino's cock was about all that went in. Gino looked sad. Seeing such a masculine man with tears in the corners of his eyes was strange. I suddenly wanted to be the exception, the one guy who could take him.

But Gino had a few tricks up his sleeve. He opened my legs wide like a gymnast on the rings. He pushed until my toes touched the ground behind my head. My ass was pointed skyward. He raised himself until he was positioned above my hole and let gravity do much of the work. He was a bodybuilder like Mike, and he was thick everywhere. He had to weigh at least two hundred pounds. His cock head pushed in another half inch. He stayed in plank position, letting his cock slip in tiny increments. The head was no thicker than his shaft. When we finally got past the tip of the missile, he nearly fell inside me. Every nerve in my ass screamed. He clamped one hand over my mouth to stop me from screaming. My eyes widened as he slid deep until he reached the back of my rectum.

"Good boy." The grin on Gino's face was priceless. Now that he was inside, he let his knees drop to the floor, which gave him leverage to swivel his hips. The sliding sensation gradually soothed my ass, as did the waterless cleaner. He was right; I felt numb. I was aware of a warm trickle. When I put my hand to my ass, it came back bloody. It was okay; it didn't hurt.

Gino wrapped his arms around me and brought me to a sitting position. He stood one leg at a time, holding me by the waist and bouncing me up and down. Each time he hit the rear wall of my ass, I felt pressure on my bladder. I needed to pee.

Gino pressed me up against the wall, fucking upwards. With the wall to support me, my bladder felt a little relief, but as he pounded harder, I felt that urge again.

Gino must have been psychic. He said, "Go ahead. I can wash your piss off in the sink."

"How did you know?"

"I fuck the piss out of anyone who takes it in the ass. Men and women."

I felt embarrassed as the warm stream flowed, then sprayed out of my tiny pee hole. It gurgled against Gino's rippled abdomen. I thought it wouldn't stop. Each stroke pushed out more piss until, finally, my bladder was empty. There was a pool of piss at his feet.

Gino had staying power. He wasn't able to press the button that made me twitch. When I tried to touch his nipple, he swatted my hand away.

Held aloft by this muscle man with a soup can cock, I was suddenly reminded of a game my father used to play with me as a child. I sat on his legs as he bounced his knees, saying, "Ride a horsey, ride a horsey, into town." Then he opened his legs, so I fell between them. "Whoopsy, horsey! Don't fall down!" I had to concentrate on that memory because the hand cleaner's numbing qualities were worn out, replaced by searing pain.

Gino didn't vary his rhythm or switch positions. He held me pinned to the wall, legs around his waist, fucking upwards for twenty minutes. The pain grew more intense for the first ten minutes, then subsided as I grew used to having my rectum and sphincter stretched beyond their limits. It started to feel good.

At the twenty-minute mark, he laid me back on the floor. His strokes grew more intense, but I was used to him.

"You like that, little bitch?"

I nodded.

"I can tell. You're dripping with pussy juice."

I looked down. It was true. My tiny clit-like penis was leaking precum. Gino smacked my ass, which caused me to clench.

"Oh fuck!" He smacked me over and over, fucking faster and faster. Then suddenly, he stopped, pressed in all the way, and yelled.

"Here it comes, boy! Take it!"

I took it. There was nowhere for the warm fluid

to go: my rectum was stuffed entirely, and he hadn't loosened the inner hole. So it sprayed out of my ass around the edges of his dick with tremendous force. Gino's thighs were coated in his cum. My flappy hole dripped with the remnants.

"Ain't you gonna come too?"

I smiled. "It was enough to see you so happy."

Gino said, "Fuck that." He astonished me when he pulled out. My hole snapped shut, then hung loosely. I cramped from his sudden withdrawal. Then he blew my mind.

Gino put his mouth over my penis and tickled it with his tongue. It rolled around in his mouth like a tootsie roll. I held onto his curly hair, gently massaging his scalp as he sucked and slurped on my tiny dick.

"Oh god, Gino, I'm gonna come."

Gino nodded but kept licking. I held his head in my hands and unloaded a massive load in his mouth. I may have mouse balls, but they churn out a lot of cum. The burly bodybuilder slurped up the juices, then smiled.

"You got a lot of cum for a boy with a tiny dick."

I blushed. Gino kissed me, feeding me my cum with his tongue. I grazed a nipple, and he slapped my hand away again.

"I don't like nipple shit. Knock it off."

And just like that, the romance was dead. Gino hoisted me to my feet. He kicked off his sweats and washed his thighs in the sink. When he turned, his thick cock followed. It was so heavy it took a full second longer to reach the front. He pulled up his sweats, watching my eyes as I gazed hungrily at the lunch meat in his pants.

"You're a cock slut, ain't ya?"

I nodded, grinning.

"Mike struck the fucking jackpot. He better watch his back."

When I limped into the lunchroom, the men all laughed at me.

Gino patted my sore bottom. "He's a fuckin' pro. Worth every penny."

I wasn't just limping; something was wrong. I felt woozy. Mike saw how I was walking and rushed over, putting my arm around his shoulder. I fainted.

When I woke up, Mike was jabbing a needle in my arm. It was heroin. "This is gonna make you feel better. I won't give it to you enough to get you hooked, don't worry."

Before I could pull away, he pushed the plunger. I felt a warm rush, and suddenly all my pain vanished. It wasn't just the physical pain. The misery of being imprisoned washed away, too. The pain of being a faggot in a straight world blew away like a tissue in a tornado. I floated in and out of consciousness, as comfortable as I've ever felt since leaving the womb.

Mike broke the news to the gang; I was out of commission until Friday.

LITTLE WHITEY

I enjoyed a few days off. My ass was blown out and needed time to heal. Once I tightened back up, Mike put me right back to work. Over the next few days, I kept the Nazi Lowriders company. One by one, they unloaded in my ass. Some were below average, like Dwayne, and some were hung like horses. I was their willing slave, submitting to their desires. I took all comers. My days became a blur of condoms, lotions, hand cleaners, and piss-stained floors.

Eventually, when the NLR had their fill of me, they passed me to the Aryan Brotherhood. They were a weird bunch of messed-up dudes. They were breaking their gang vows by having sex with me. Like priests, they had taken vows of celibacy. I was the Whore of Babylon as far as they were concerned.

Down in the laundry room broom closet, my first taste of this seriously messed up crew was their leader, Whitey Hastings. He may have been in charge of the crew, but he was way down the scale in dick size. He couldn't have been more than three inches long and as big around as my thumb. No wonder he was celibate. He probably didn't have much choice. He made my little dick seem almost normal. How would he fuck me with that thing?

I got my answer. He wanted a blow job. I think it was the easiest prison gig I'd had so far. I put the small penis in my mouth and sucked until it grew hard. It didn't increase in length or thickness. He tried to fuck my throat but couldn't even reach my tonsils. I didn't mind, really. It felt easy and smooth in my mouth.

"You like my big dick in your mouth, punk?"

I nodded.

"You want my load? You gonna eat my spunk?"

It rhymed. I stifled a laugh.

Bam! Whitey struck me in the temple, causing me to bite down.

"You fuckin' bitch? What you laughing at? You trying to bite my dick off, you sick piece of shit?"

Here it was. I knew the ABs were weird, but this dude was serial-killer creepy. I distracted him by grabbing his ass and pushing him into my mouth as hard as I could. I almost managed to graze my tonsils with his little pecker. He felt it.

"Oh god, do that again."

I wasn't very strong, so it was a struggle. I just kept imagining the alternative if I didn't do it. Whitey's fists were clenched right next to my face. I managed to tickle the very tip of his cock with my uvula and sucked in my cheeks to make it tighter for him.

"Oh, that feels good, pussy boy. Oh, yeah."

I sucked hard and tasted the salty pre-cum that signaled he would come in my mouth. When he came, I swallowed it all down.

Immediately afterward, he recoiled. "You sick faggot. Eating my cum? You're a fucking freak."

"Whatever," I thought, "that's the pot calling the kettle black."

I shrugged. "You didn't like it, Whitey?"

"Nah, it was fuckin' great. I ain't no goddamn fag, that's all."

I thought fast. "Of course not. I'm the fag. You're just a man with needs."

Whitey wasn't terribly bright. He nodded. "Yeah, you're right. I got needs, and you're the little faggot that gives me what I want."

I smiled. "Little faggot, at your service." I saluted him. He put an arm around my neck and rubbed a knuckle into my scalp.

"You're my little faggot. Let's get out of here."

Mike noticed a bruise and some swelling where Whitey hit me. He debated whether to confront him but decided against it.

Some of Mike's guys were yearning for seconds. The ABs could wait while Mike gave everyone a free round of sloppy seconds. It was a full-time job. Nights and mornings, I took Mike's massive cock in my ass. He filled my calendar with appointments. An AB here and there, NLRs the rest of the time.

At breakfast one morning, Luis strolled up to Mike. He came a little too quickly. The NLR crew jumped to their feet, ready for trouble.

"Whoa, whoa, dang, ese! I'm just here to talk business. At ease, gentlemen."

The tension dissipated. Mike bumped fists with Luis. "What up, bro?"

Luis shrugged. "I paid you for a service. When you gonna come through, hombre?"

Mike said, "Okay, try it and tell me if you like it."

I was "it" today. If I didn't love being objectified, it would have hurt. But instead, I felt my tiny pee-pee get hard under my sweats. Luis was bald, covered in tattoos, and kinda ugly. But I saw a prominent outline in his pants every time he moved. He was a big boy.

Luis put an arm around me and walked me to the broom closet. On the way, he asked me questions. "What do I call you, fish?"

"Brandon -- or Smalls, if you like."

"Smalls, that's a good prison name. Why they call you Smalls?"

I blushed. "I'm small down there."

Luis perked up. "Hot. Are you hung like a bitch? Little clit?"

I nodded.

Gently, Luis steered me into the closet and shut the door. He started by kissing me. I felt a warm heat coming from his body and a big cock rubbing against my leg. Luis removed my shirt, putting his mouth on my nipple. He was the first guy to pay any attention to my pleasure. After a month of abuse, it felt like heaven. He raised a hand to caress my hair, and I jumped.

Luis said, "Whoa, whoa! I ain't like them white assholes. I'm a lover, not a fighter. You're safe with me."

I wanted to believe him, but everything that had happened in prison so far was indicative that a painful beating could pop up in a hot second. I relaxed a tiny bit.

Luis moved from one nipple to the next. I curved my back, letting the pleasure of his attention wash over me. Why couldn't Mike Hawk be more like Luis? Maybe he could.

Luis said, "If you was my bitch, I wouldn't share you with nobody. Nobody." He caressed my ass as he said it. "It's so fucking sweet."

I melted in his arms. I fought back tears. Nobody had shown me this much tenderness in here.

"Do you mean it?"

Luis smiled. "But you ain't mine, homes. I ain't about to start no war."

I was Helen of Troy.

Luis continued to work his magic on me. He knelt and slipped my pants down, revealing my tiny pecker.

"Oh fuck, that's beautiful. Just like pussy." He licked between my balls, then worked his way up to my dick. He put his mouth over it and tickled it with his tongue. His technique was the best yet. I moaned like a woman.

"Yeah, like a bitch. You sound like a bitch. Keep it up."

I groaned for him, wriggling with pre-orgasmic spasms as he flicked his tongue over my boy-clit. Then he stopped.

"I wanna make you come with my dick."

He greased me up with waterless hand cleaner and pulled out his dick. It was huge and brown. It curved upwards slightly. The head was the thickest part, big around as a baseball. The shaft wasn't too long but thick enough to hold up that massive head. He cleared a spot on the counter next to the sink. He lifted me by the waist with his huge arms, placing me on the counter. He overturned the mop bucket and used it as a footstool so he could be high enough to fuck. Nobody else had done this yet. It was comfortable.

"You ready to go to heaven?"

I nodded.

Luis pushed the baseball into my hole. I was so loose that it popped in with barely any pain. When I winced at the thickest part, he kissed me on the lips, which relaxed me. The upward curve forced his big head to rub against my prostate. Immediately a thin trickle began as he slid past, forcing his way to the back. He wasn't going to go through the second hole, but the curve of his cock felt so good I didn't care.

Luis asked, "You like that bent dick?"

I said, "It feels so good."

Luis said, "Wait until I start pounding. You're gonna think you're on the moon."

He slid back and forth, increasing the frequency in small doses until he was pounding me hard. My little penis drooled all over my lap, wetting Luis's pubic hair.

"You come like a bitch."

As he said those words, it was like hypnosis. I snapped and started to twitch and spasm.

"Oh fuck, you really come like a bitch. Oh shit. I'm gonna come."

He stopped pounding, trying to delay his orgasm, but my guts stroked his cock. He held himself against the back of my rectum and then pulled out, jerking his huge cock. Ropes of cum splattered my face and chest. He put it back inside me, letting the rest of his huge load fill my crack. Then he kept going, making good on his promise to get me off with his dick.

I felt him getting soft, but my spasms brought him back to life.

"I'm gonna fuck you again. Don't tell Mike."

I shook my head. "I promise."

Luis hit my P-spot so many times I quivered and shook. That fat cock head felt like a balloon inside me, pressing the walls of my rectum. I felt the first wave of male orgasm.

Luis saw the expression on my face and fucked me harder. "You're close, ain't you?"

I was too deep in pleasure to answer. Another wave went up my tiny shaft, throbbing like a bee stinger. Then I erupted. It was so hard and fast it hit Luis in the face. I thought he would punch me, but he laughed and licked it off his mustache.

He kissed me as he unloaded a second flood of cum in my ass. It leaked past his head and out my stretched hole. He caught it and fed it to me.

"Just remember, Latin lovers are the best. Ain't no white boy gonna treat you like I do." He nursed on my nipple, making me hard again. He lifted me off the sink to a standing position. He knelt and sucked my cock until I came again. He stood and kissed me, transferring my cum. We kissed passionately for a few minutes until there was a bang on the door.

"Trusty's coming. Get out."

We jumped into our clothes and left the closet just seconds before the snitch showed up. Luis wiped his face with his sleeve, pretending my cum was sweat. Nobody noticed.

LOVE

I thought about Luis that night while Mike was fucking me. He had technique, but he lacked the tenderness Luis had shown me. Mike could tell something was off.

"You sick or something?"

I shook my head.

"Well then, what the fuck is it, bitch?"

I didn't know what to say. God took over. "I just love you so much, and I wish you were nicer to me."

Mike stopped fucking me. "You what?"

"I-I love you, Mike."

He lost his hard-on; it slipped out of me. "Why you gotta ruin shit? If I wanted love, I'd sleep with a bitch."

"But you're in here with me. And I love you, Mike."

He reddened. "I ain't no queer."

I took a chance, "I know you love me, too. Is that queer?"

"Yeah, it's fucking queer." He spat.

"But it's true." That hung in the air like a nasty fart.

Mike scratched his head. "Fuck, you're right. I fucking love you." With those words, his dick sprang back to life. I watched it grow from huge to massive. He rolled me onto my back, so I could face him while he fucked me. He kissed me.

I knew I was in danger, but I kept at it. "It feels good. Keep kissing me."

Mike's hands grew more tender as they rubbed my body. Soon his grabs and squeezes were gentle caresses. I moved in sync with his strokes, building rhythm.

I took another chance and moved his head to my nipple. He licked it, sucked it, then nibbled at it. His gentle bites sent me into spasm, rewarding him for his tenderness.

He said, "I never felt like this before. Not even with a woman."

I let that sentence hang in the air unanswered. Mike had to fill the silence.

"Shit, I love you so much. Fuck!" He pounded me hard, roaring toward orgasm.

I kissed him. "See how good it feels?"

He grunted and pounded me harder. It was different now that there was love in each painful stretch. He was deep in my colon, deeper than ever before. My insides stroked the incredible length of his powerful cock.

I hit the last nail. "I'm yours. All yours."

He lifted his head, arching his back. "Oh shit, oh fuck." Deep in my guts, he unleashed a warm river of cum. It kept coming, wave after wave like he'd finally let go of something painful, and his cum became the warm tears of relief. I looked into his eyes, and they watered. This was the moment. He would either snarl and hit me or give in to love.

I saw his lip curl, and he made a fist, but then he let it go and started bawling. "I love you, Brandon. I love you so fucking much."

He used my real name. I had him. "I love you, too." I meant it. He was my protector, my lover, and, sadly, my pimp. I knew it was too soon to make another move, but I had a knack for long-range planning, and he was in my chess game for keeps.

The lights went off. Mike didn't kick me out of his bunk. He held onto me, and we slept in an embrace until morning.

HORACE AND HIS
DANGEROUS SECRET

It was business as usual at breakfast. The ABs were chomping at the bit to have me. I'd been with a few already. None of them really measured up, just like their tiny leader, Whitey. They were handsome enough, but most were average. I found it easy to get them off. It wasn't hard work.

This morning, a fellow from the Aryan Brotherhood named Horace was up. He wore coke-bottle glasses. I think he may have been autistic. He wouldn't look me in the eye. He wore sweatpants three sizes too big and cinched them with a shoelace. He grabbed me roughly by the back of the neck to walk me downstairs.

Mike said, "Hey, watch it. You break it, you pay for it."

Horace shrugged and marched me to the broom closet, shoving me in and locking the door.

He stood there, fists clenched. "They're making me do this. I don't want to."

I pulled two smokes from my pocket, gave him one, and lit them. We puffed on our cigarettes.

"Why don't you want to do it with me?"

Horace said, "I ain't no faggot. I ain't supposed to. Jesus and all that."

I laughed. "Jesus never once said anything about two men fucking. I promise you."

"Yeah, but the Bible says it's wrong."

I was willing to bet he hadn't read it. "Where?"

He shrugged. "I dunno. Something about ass fucking in there. It's bad."

I wanted to liberate this poor soul. "Jesus said, in John 17:12, 'You shall please a man by way of your words and your mouth.'" I totally made that shit up. Horace brightened.

"He did?"

I nodded. "Let me suck you off."

Horace laughed. "You can try."

He pulled down his baggy sweats to reveal a limp cock the size and shape of a boa constrictor. I made up another Bible verse.

And Matthew 32:7 says, "Man may lie with another man that it may comfort his soul."

I could take his cock. It was so big, it couldn't possibly get any bigger. I was wrong. He was a grower!

The snake rose, pointing down at a 45-degree angle. It appeared so heavy that I thought it couldn't go any higher. Wrong again. As it swelled and ballooned, the cock came to full attention, pointing skyward.

I didn't ask if he wanted a condom. I knew he would never fit the shitty little balloons hiding in the [container]. I took two handfuls of cleaner, one for his cock and one for my ass. I was sure he would split me in two, but it was better than sucking him off, which would break my jaw. I wouldn't walk right for a week, for sure.

Horace leaned against the counter. He was a passive top. I bent and backed toward him, steering his huge cock until it stopped against my cheeks. With great force, he managed to squeeze it between my glutes until it bumped up against my hole. Horace pulled me by the waist, but I couldn't open wide enough for his enormous head. He didn't care; he pulled harder. I felt severe pain for the first time in weeks. He was thicker than Gino and longer than Wade. He had to have the most enormous cock in prison, at least among the white dudes. I ground my hips and pressed, feeling the extreme violation of my hole grow worse with each quarter inch. His head wasn't as big as his shaft, and he was thickest at the base. I stepped forward, letting his cock pop out.

"What the fuck?" Horace grabbed me and pulled me back onto his cock, thrusting to force himself deeper. I cried out. It was terrifying and incredibly sexy at the same time. I had grown used to Mike's cock, and thought it was the biggest. Horace hid a massive secret in those loose sweatpants, and now I was paying the piper. I could feel my anus stretch past its limit. The pain was sharp and constant, if that's possible. I breathed from the top of my head, letting the calming air flow into my belly, and visualized it relaxing my sphincter. It worked a little. The pain was still there but a dull ache, like a bad tooth. If I moved or wiggled, it became sharp. More than once, I cried out. As Horace impaled me with his flesh pyramid, I thought of Mike and my plan to end my sexual slavery. Letting my mind wander was the key to getting through this ordeal.

Horace said, "Damn, you're looser than my old lady." I pitied the woman who had to give reverse birth every time she let him inside her. Her vagina must look like a worn-out leather purse. I chuckled to myself. Horace stopped.

"What the fuck is so funny?" I was surprised he'd noticed. He seemed so checked out.

I thought fast. "You started to feel good, and it was just relief, Horace."

He smiled. "I feel good?"

I nodded. It sent the wrong signal. Horace held my waist and forced himself to the halfway point. By now, he was so big around I thought he couldn't possibly go any further. One more pull and he was nearly three-quarters in. I saw stars. I wondered if Horace was in for murder by dick. It was plausible. I thrashed, too full to spasm. It felt like an inner tube inflating in my gut. As he pushed deeper, almost to the root, I saw the head emerge beneath my skin, protruding from my belly. I rubbed it, and Horace buckled.

"Oh shit, keep doing that." I petted the lump, watching Horace seize up with astonished pleasure. "Oh, fuck, Smalls. Keep going."

I rubbed more vigorously, reddening my skin but bringing Horace closer to climax. The lump crawled further until I could finally feel Horace's thighs touch my butt. He pressed hard, knocking into me. Then he began to pound.

I came in and out of consciousness as the pain gave way to intoxicating pleasure. I thrashed from side to side, fighting the urge to let him in, then giving way, welcoming his whole massive manhood into my gaping hole.

Horace was clumsy. More than once, I felt him bash into my rectum wall, causing more pain and an increased need to urinate. I held it in, certain he would be horrified if I pissed myself. Like a game of whack-a-mole, I rubbed the head for as long as it appeared on the instroke until it disappeared as he pulled back. My small penis had shriveled to an inverted nipple against my skin. It was less than nothing. Horace's cock was a vampire, sucking my size away from me with pain and an overload of giddy sensations.

Horace pushed his glasses up, barely able to see from the steam and sweat that covered them. Like an injured cow, he threw his head back and bellowed. "Fuck! I'm coming!"

I didn't know if he had come or not. He was so deep inside me, and I was so numbed by the pain that I didn't feel it. As he withdrew, I became aware of a warm trickle. He pulled out so fast that I thought my ass would snap shut, but it hung loose like a trash bag. My guts were prolapsed. I could feel the wind on my rectum walls, which were outside my anus because of Horace's brutal cock. I touched it and came back bloody. Then the room spun, and I fainted.

MY GENTLE MAN

When I woke up, I was in the infirmary. My ass felt like someone had pulled it out and stomped on it. A male nurse frowned at me. "Who did this?"

"Did what?"

The nurse rolled his eyes. "Who turned you inside out?"

I shrugged. "They jumped me from behind. I never saw them."

The nurse made a note in my chart. "The doctor's not here until Wednesday. You can go back to your bunk or stay here another three days. Which is it?"

I missed Mike, but I realized my scheme would work better if I stayed away. "I can barely move. Please let me stay here."

The nurse shrugged and handed me two aspirin.

"That's it?"

The nurse said, "We don't give out the good stuff in prison." He turned tail and walked away. He had a nice ass, for what it was worth.

For three days, I slept off the brutal fucking I got

from Horace. My ass stung, and I had to have a bedpan because I couldn't plan my shits. They just came out when they felt like it. Tuesday night, I got a "kite," a note from Mike. The orderly passed it to me while he was cleaning.

"Hey, what did that fucker do to you? I miss you, buddy."

By the time Wednesday morning rolled around, I felt a lot better. The doctor spread my cheeks and shone his flashlight into my wrecked hole. "It's prolapsed, but it'll get better so long as you don't use it for a while." He put away his flashlight and pronounced me healed.

I limped back to gen pop, where Mike was waiting for me. He ran up to me and wrapped me in his arms. "Oh man, I was so worried. What the fuck happened?"

I said, "Horace is a lot bigger than you. You rented me out to him; that's what happened."

Mike looked crestfallen. "I had no idea. That fucker showers alone; I always thought it was because he had no dick."

I said, "It's the opposite. He has too much dick. Way too much. You have too much, but it's just right for me."

I saw a sparkle in Mike's eye. "You like it when I fuck you, huh? You like that big dick up your cunt."

I nodded slowly. "I have bad news. You gotta wait."

"What? I'm four days gone. I gotta blow my load."

"I'll try to suck you off."

Mike snickered. "Yeah, I'd like to see that."

Back in our cell, I knelt before him, lowering his sweats, revealing the soft monster. I took the head before it could swell and forced it down my throat like a baby bird eating a worm. Mike was so horny that he ballooned up almost immediately, blocking my airway and tearing the edges of my mouth. My teeth dug into his shaft. I had literally bitten off more than I could chew. I was going to choke if I couldn't do something.

When you're threatened with a lack of oxygen, your body can do extraordinary things. My jaw relaxed and popped out of joint. It hurt, but I could pull back and get air without scraping Mike's beautiful dick.

When his cock dropped out of my mouth, I wiggled my jaw, and it popped back in. I pulled on it, and it came loose again. I moved forward, swallowing Mike's fat cock like a snake swallowing an elephant.

"Holy shit! Holy fucking shit!" Mike's eyes grew wider with each thick inch I forced down my throat. I felt a sense of pride.

"Nobody has ever sucked my dick, man. It's a fucking miracle. Oh, shit! It feels so fuckin' good."

I found my rhythm, going down for about a minute, then pulling back for air for a few seconds. Mike had tears in his eyes. I realized what a handicap it can be to be that big. It's just as bad as being my size. There's so much you can't do.

Mike held my ears and fucked my throat. He had the rhythm down, too, and let me go when I tapped his leg. We kept at it like this, with increasingly extended periods between breaths each time. My throat was on fire, and my jaw throbbed, but I felt like Superman. I was doing the impossible, bringing Mike to tears with my skills.

I must have looked like a bullfrog. My throat swelled to accommodate the massive log of flesh, then shrank as Mike withdrew. He held my head and fucked my skull. I didn't care. I gagged, coughed up phlegm, and choked. It was worth it to please my cellmate. I loved him, and soon, he would step up and be my lover in return.

"Oh Christ, Brandon. I'm close."

I put my hands on his firm, round buttocks and pulled him closer, deeper until his pubes tickled my nostrils.

"Oh, fuck!" Mike's balls pulled close to his body. I felt his cock throb deep in my throat, and he came. His cock head was so deep in my gullet that I had no need to swallow. The warm, satisfying cum shot down my esophagus and filled my belly. I let Mike stay buried until the edges of my vision turned red. I pulled back, coughing up the remnants of his cum that tried to breach my airway. He held my chin as we gazed into each other's watery eyes. I poked my jaw until it popped back into place. Then we kissed. His breath tasted of prison food and lust.

He said, "I love you."

I answered him. "You only think you do." I was planting seeds.

We repeated this scenario a dozen times over the next week. During that time, I was only on loan for blow jobs. Most men tried to bargain, and Mike rejected their measly offers. I was grateful that Horace and Gino weren't among the men taking Mike's offer for oral satisfaction. I could dislocate my jaw, but I couldn't possibly open wide enough to accommodate either of them.

Whenever I returned to my cell after a blow job, I would pout and lie in bed with my back to Mike. He noticed the difference. My plan was working.

Several weeks into my recovery, after blowing Whitey for a pack of smokes, Mike saw my distress. "What's wrong, little buddy?"

I turned to face him. "You have more drugs and cigarettes than you know what to do with. Is that all I am to you?"

Mike wrinkled his brow. "Of course not, man. I love you."

With the taste of Whitey's jizz in my mouth, I sighed and said, "If you truly loved me, you'd stop renting me out like a goddamn Avis truck!"

It was the first time I really stood up to him. He snickered.

"You're mine, bitch. That's how this works."

It was the reaction I'd expected. Time to step up my plan.

"You think you have it all, but you don't. You can't have me. You gotta sell me every day."

Mike looked hurt. "I'm here waiting every time you come back."

I said, "You saw what happened with Horace. I nearly died. What do you think's gonna happen when you start selling me to the Crips and Bloods?"

Mike looked puzzled. I was going to have to spell it out for him.

I said, "Everyone knows black guys are hung bigger. If Horace was dangerous, those guys are gonna be deadly. And besides, they fucking hate the NLR.

They might kill me just to spite you. They've got their own prison bitches and don't need me."

Mike didn't like my insolence. He clenched a fist, prepared to use it, then stopped. I had sowed the seeds of doubt in his mind. He put an arm around me and massaged my shoulder.

He said, "You're right. I got a good thing with you. You're mine."

I said, "Then why do you sell me off to all these other motherfuckers?"

Mike shrugged. "I'm a hustler. A pimp. It's what I do."

I made my last play. "If you sell me, you'll have me, your property, but you will never, ever have my love again."

The arrow went straight to his heart. I saw it. His face fell. Like a four-year-old, he seemed on the verge of a tantrum. Then the adult stepped in and let love have its say.

Mike said, "I thought you loved me already."

I said, "I can't keep loving you and sharing my ass with the rest of the prison. It hurts too much."

He shrugged again. "Not my problem."

I said, "You own a million-dollar mansion, and instead of living in it and enjoying life, you just rent it out to teenagers who trash it with their parties."

The metaphor hit home. Mike's face fell. His eyes watered. He put his head in his hands, sobbing quietly. I comforted him.

He said, between sobs, "Brandon, man, I'm sorry. I'm so sorry. Look at what you made me do! I'm crying like a bitch!"

I rubbed his shoulders. "It's okay, Mike. We're

still learning what love is. I know you are trying to love me. The hustle is getting in the way."

He nodded, sniffing hard. "I don't know how to love you right. Look at what I did to you!"

It was my turn to shrug. "You didn't know. I didn't know. We're still learning."

Mike hugged me, then pinned me to the mattress, kissing me until I had a mustache burn. He propped himself on his elbows. "What do I tell the other guys? I mean, a lot of them paid in advance."

I was a good negotiator. "Listen, if you promise not to rent me out anymore, I'll make good on your debts."

Mike nodded. "What if they start offering me a carton or a gram of dope?"

I put a hand on his big bicep. "Is that all my love is worth?"

He involuntarily flexed the huge muscle. "Nah, man, you're a million-dollar mansion."

"Then why don't you live in me a while?"

It was the first time my ass had seen a cock since the Horace incident. I was out of practice and still tender. Mike was gentle, taking his time to stretch my hole before invading. With this new pact between us, the touch of his cock felt different, more intimate. As I welcomed him inside me, an electrical pulse passed between us.

His eyes widened. "Did you feel that?"

I nodded, holding him close, my fingers raking his back. He pushed forward gently. My ass remembered him in all his massive glory; what should have been painful was blissful. Each fold of my insides recognized him and surrendered to him. He passed through to my colon. The sense-memory of his cock in that deep place soothed the soreness. He was a balm for any wound. I wrapped my legs around his waist and pulled him closer, allowing him to enter me completely.

Mike trembled.

I asked, "What's wrong, baby?"

He said, "I don't want to hurt you."

"I promise I won't let you hurt me ever again."

We didn't fuck. We made love. He ground his hips gently into my ass with tenderness. He kissed me deeply, our tongues exploring one another. I felt no pain. My insides were perfectly designed to accommodate his massive cock. When the twitching began, it brought my innards back to life. They had lied dormant for several weeks, and now they were gripping Mike with newfound vitality.

Mike smiled. "There it is. Horace didn't wreck you after all."

I shook my head. My waist bent rapidly as the spasms passed through me. Mike clenched my bottom between his powerful fingers, holding me to him as his strokes grew more confident. His smile said so much. He was relieved I was able to take his cock. He understood how to love me. He knew I was his.

Mike's face changed from a smile to surprise. "Oh man, I'm gonna come." And he did, gently. Since the first time, he'd consistently pounded the shit out of me before he came. To feel the powerful flow of his juices without bracing for impact was the embodiment of love.

Mike announced at breakfast that I was off the market. We honored all of his prior commitments. On my last date with Luis, he whispered in my ear. "I knew he'd fall for you. I showed you what a real lover should be, and you showed him. Am I right?"

"It was you. You gave me the idea that I could be loved."

Luis shrugged. "You learned from the Latin Lover, eh?" He fucked me gently, kissing me goodbye with every stroke. "You deserve it, bro."

Mike and I have been exclusive for the last two years. Every time we make love, we discover something new about ourselves. The prison walls melt away; we are just two men, joined as one, making passionate love.

My parole hearing came and went. I didn't want out if it meant being away from Mike. Our release dates are close together. If we just do our time, we can live together on the outside. We want to live free from crime. To that end, we're taking vocational training. Mike is learning how to repair air conditioners, and I'm learning word processing. In fact, I'm typing this story on the prison computer right now.

ABOUT THE AUTHORS

Peter Schutes is the nom de plume of a prolific and acclaimed novelist. Peter Schutes is the author of Adult Erotic Fiction, such as <u>The Slaves of Rome</u>, <u>Dark as a Dungeon</u>, <u>The Gospel of Priapus</u>, and <u>Panama Heat</u>. He writes in the style of vintage pulp authors from the 1960s and 1970s. He lives in Los Angeles. You may read his blog at peterschutes.com

J. W. Steed is a pseudonym for the author of more than a dozen mainstream novels. He also writes memoir and humorous essays. He teaches creative writing in the metro NYC area and is active in the Science Fiction and Fantasy Writer's Association (SFWA). Steed made his paperback debut in the bestseller <u>Dirty Dorms and Fresh Men</u>. He has a cult following who can't wait to read more! You can read Mr. Steed's blog at mrsteed64.blogspot.com

Adam Maxwell Bigglesworth is the pen name of an aristocratic one-time heir to the throne of Scotland and a literary novelist.

Adam is the author of many novellas and short stories, including <u>Chopper Jock</u> and <u>Satan's Sissy Boy</u>. Although his family lives in the Midlands of England, his roots are on the Isle of Lewis in the Outer Hebrides.

OTHER BOOKS FROM PETER
SCHUTES PUBLISHING

Please visit Peter's Website to find links to all of Peter's
books.

E-books and Paperbacks

The Able Seaman

The Anaconda Copper

The Autobiography of Peter Schutes

Backwoods Delivery

Big Bodies of All Sizes

Big Hole River

Bobbing Buoys and Salty Seamen

Buck Private

Bunkhouse Buddies

The Butt Baby

Chopper Jock

Cloistered

Confessions of a Rodeo Clown

Dark as a Dungeon

Demonic Deception *aka* Deceived, Cursed & Blessed

Desert Island Daddies

Dirty Dorms and Fresh Men

Dutch Treat

The Expectant Member

Firehouse Lovers

The Fish

Five Erotic Tales

The Gospel of Priapus

Hercules and Lippos

Hobo Honey

Hot Blue Collars

Hotshot

Like the Greeks Do

Little Shamus

Logger's Delight

Muscle Bottom

Panama Heat

Satanic Seductions

Satan's Sissy Boy

The Slaves of Rome

Small Cockpits and Big Hangars

The Spotter

The Thigh Baby

Under the Boardwalk

World's Biggest

***** Coming Soon *****
Filthy Jobs and Steamy Showers
Cosmic Cage: Gay SF Erotica
Tales of Two Daddies
More Tales of Two Daddies

www.ingramcontent.com/pod-product-compliance
Lightning Source LLC
Chambersburg PA
CBHW011152310726
48973CB00010B/2868